So it's their stronghold, their sanctum city, and no one has been able to put them down in Chicago. But the mob has to be shown that there are no sanctuaries in this war. I'm hitting Chicago and it's going to be a wipeout . . . them or me. It matters, somewhere, which side wins. The universe cares. I consign my fate to the needs of the universe.

And I consign the Mafia TO HELL!

—Mack Bolan, THE EXECUTIONER

THE EXECUTIONER:
Chicago Wipeout

PINNACLE BOOKS • NEW YORK CITY

DEDICATION

The deeper responsibilities of life are eternally found beyond the self; human values are sometimes dignified only by a willingness to fight for them. This book is dedicated to all of the good fighters everywhere.

If this life be not a real fight, in which something is eternally gained for the universe by success, it is no better than a game of private theatricals from which one may withdraw at will.

Man's character is his fate. —Heraclitus

PROLOGUE

Mack Bolan knew what he was walking into at Chicago. There were no illusions of his own invincibility, and certainly no misjudgement of enemy power in this stronghold of organized crime. This was the city that the mob owned, the self-professed crime capital of the Western World, the locale of the mob's deepest entrenchment anywhere. And Bolan's challenge was knowingly hurled into the teeth of that vast empire which was characterized by *The Chicago Tribune* as:

A world in which wrong is right—in which all incentive for honor, justice, suppression of crime, and even fundamental discipline has disappeared from broad divisions of the police department, the courts, and the all-pervading political party machine that has a strangle-hold on Chicago proper.

What sort of man would single-handedly invade such a province of power with the intention of subduing it, of "shaking their house down," of breaking the chains which had held this city captive for decades? What motivates a man like Mack Bolan—how does an ordinary young man become transformed into a methodical death-machine pledged to wholesale slaughter and unending warfare?

The truth of this particular case seems that, simply, there was no "transformation"—Bolan appears to be the same man in Chicago that he was in Pittsfield, scene of his original confrontation with the Mafia. The same skills which had carried him safely through two years of combat in Southeast Asia were moving him through this new jungle of violence and terror. The same scorn of death that had accompanied him into deep penetrations of enemy territory in Vietnam had walked with him into the enclaves of syndicated corruption and criminal power.

It should not be concluded that Bolan was a "wild ass warrior" who recklessly stormed a superior enemy in suicidal attacks. He had a contempt for *death,* not for life. He did not fling his life into the hands of the gods and demand a safe passage; Bolan possessed a genius for warfare and had the combat instincts of a battle-hardened soldier. He also had a knack for equalizing the balance of power between himself and his enemies. This professional soldier was entirely human, and subject to all the dreams, desires and anxieties of any normal human being.

Perhaps the most revealing insight into the character of this warrior was provided by an ex-army buddy with whom he became re-involved during his French adventure. Wilson Brown told Bolan, at the height of the Riviera rampage, "You know, I guess what I dig about you, man, is your *guts* . . . you've got a weird combination there, Sarge—tough guts and warm heart. Most cats don't know how to carry both."

Tough guts and warm heart, and indeed Bolan knew how to carry both at the same time. On many occasions in Vietnam he had jeopardized his own life and mission to provide emergency assistance to stricken villagers. Though he had earned his tag, *The Executioner,* through his proficiency as a military sniper, he had also been quietly recognized among local medics as *Sergeant Mercy,* the guy who seldom returned from a penetration strike without one or several wounded or sick Vietnamese civilians in his care, usually children.

This facet of Mack Bolan had carried over to his war on the Mafia. Though he was one of the most wanted "criminals" in America, he had never engaged police authority in a shootout, and there is no record of harm befalling innocent bystanders as a result of an Executioner "hit." He planned his operations with great care to insure that only the deserving tasted his war. On various occasions, he broke off and retreated when it became obvious that such conditions could not be met; often these retreats were undertaken at great personal hazard.

In any composite picture of Bolan the man, a central and unshakeable fact emerges: this is a man responding to a high call to duty—and with this response costing him everything that had ever held meaning for his life. No kill-crazy goon, no mentally-disturbed victim of combat-fatigue, no arrogant superman glorying in his power over life and death—but an often wearied and frightened and lonely and continually harassed human being who was simply doing a job that needed doing. No zealot was Bolan—his greatest enemies were his own self-doubts, which were often immense, and a frequently overpowering revulsion for this life of gore and terror.

His war had not begun on such a high plane, of course. It started as an act of simple vengeance. Bolan had been fighting the war in Vietnam when his mother, his father, and his younger sister suffered violent deaths at home, indirect victims of a Mafia loansharking operation. The grieving soldier returned home to bury his beloved dead and to learn that "the omnipotent outfit" was beyond the reach of the law. They were not, however, beyond the reach of this combat-tested "executioner." He remained in Pittsfield to take justice into his own hands in a cooly calculated campaign against the Frenchi Family, declaring, "I am not their judge. I am their judgement. I am their *executioner*."

The battle of Pittsfield (*The Executioner: War Against the Mafia*) left that Mafia arm a shambles and provided Bolan with deeper insights into the spreading menace of organized crime. In his personal journal, he had written: "It looks like I have been fighting the wrong enemy. Why defend a front line eight thousand miles away when the *real* enemy is chewing up everything you love back home? I have talked to the police about this situation and they seem to be helpless to do anything. The problem, as I see it, is that the rules of warfare are all rigged against the cops . . . what is needed here is a bit of direct action, strategically planned, and to hell with the rules. Over in 'Nam we called it a 'war of attrition.' Seek out and destroy. Exterminate the enemy. I guess it's time a war was declared on the home front. The same kind of war we've been fighting at 'Nam. The very same kind."

During the course of that "very same kind" of initial engagement, Bolan rejected the protection of a sympathetic police official and vowed unending warfare against "this greater enemy." It is problematical whether or not Bolan's vow could have strongly influenced the course of his life from that point. The fact of the matter was that the syndicate had also declared

12

Bolan dead. His name was entered upon a Mafia death certificate, or "contract," with a face value of $100,000. It was open season on Mack Bolan and the big hunt was on, with every ambitious hood and freelance gunman in the country anxious to collect the bounty. So even without a personal commitment to battle the Mafia kingdoms, Bolan would have been forced into a purely defensive mode of warfare, with lifelong flight or imprisonment as the alternatives.

While rationalizing his own position and formulating an offensive posture, Bolan allowed his jungle instincts to take over. He faded from the scene of original combat and resurfaced shortly thereafter in Los Angeles with his battle plans firmly in mind, and he recruited a squad of former combat buddies to carry this war to the new enemy. It was to follow this battle plan: "We'll hit the Mafia so fast, so often, and from so many directions they'll think hell fell on them. We steal, we kill, we terrorize, and we take every Goddamn thing they have. Then we'll see how powerful and well organized they are." (*The Executioner: Death Squad.*)

But Bolan's challenge was not only accepted by the enemy—it was taken up also by the Los Angles Police Department, and the Los Angeles battles became a personal tragedy which also revealed the full scope of this seemingly futile contest against insurmountable odds. Only partially victorious, Bolan again faded —resolving to never again involve others in his private war with the syndicate—and again he was alone, desperately seeking to evade police dragnets and with all the hounds of hell baying along his trail.

On the California desert he located another battlefield friend, now a cosmetic surgeon, who gave Bolan a new face and at least the prospect of a new

13

orientation to life. Again Bolan opted in the direction of duty, and he used the new face as another combat tool, infiltrating the inner family of Julian DiGeorge with a quiet ferocity that left this Southern California kingdom in reeling ruin. (*The Executioner: Battle Mask.*)

With the new face now as much a liability as the old one, the one-man army followed a trail from the dry sands of the southwest to the glittering beaches of Miami Beach to crash a nationwide Mafia summit conference attended by all the families of *La Cosa Nostra.* A new dimension was added to the Bolan Wars at Miami, and a new determination was forged in the mind of the man now universally feared and respected by the underworld, Mack the Bastard Bolan. (*The Executioner: Miami Massacre.*)

In this new determination, the mission was to remain alive and to carry the war continually to the enemy—to keep them frightened, to harass their programs and sneer at their delusions of grandeur, to hurl their omnipotence back into their teeth and reduce it to a trembling impotence—these were the desired effects of the new dimension of Bolan's war.

Meanwhile, remain alive. And this was not easy, with every law enforcement agency in the nation geared to his apprehension and with armies of bounty hunters swarming his trail. In this interest, Bolan unintentionally found himself in France and involved with a continental arm of the mob, and soon all of Europe (plus an American expeditionary force) was trying to crush him. (*The Executioner: Continental Contract.*) It was here that Bolan came to the realization that, "To be truly alive, you have to be ready to die for something. Harder still, there are times when you have to be willing to kill for something."

14

Bolan found that he was both ready to die and willing to kill. In an act of compassion and loyalty, he rejected the compelling tug of "Eden" and the loving arms of a dazzling French movie star to rescue a group of Parisian *joie* girls who had befriended him and were subsequently suffering from the vindictiveness of a local Mafia chieftain. Putting his war where his heart was, Bolan exposed himself to the most comprehensive threat to his existence yet undertaken as he launched a series of lightning assaults against the combined forces of international headhunters. His battle magic and utter scorn for personal danger blazed a trail of destruction across France and Bolan learned that there are "no crossovers between Hell and Eden."

When again we encountered Bolan, *The Executioner,* he was in England and searching out a homeward path. His search, however, quickly became *Assault On Soho,* and Bolan discovered that, ". . . I am living in an invisible domain of violence that follows me wherever I go." He also found that all pathways home were crossed with extreme jeopardy, and swinging Londontown very quickly began to throb to the Executioner's battlecry. Diverse forces were closing in on Bolan in England, and he learned the hard way that the Mafia held no monopoly over evil.

Nevertheless he overcame the coalition of underground power in London and dealt another mortal blow to a cancerous tentacle of Mafia influence, but not without taking on a new appreciation of fear, and disgust for this spreading menace.

He returned to New York with the personal commitment to "bust this kingdom of evil if I can live that long." But New York turned into a nightmare and an orgy of bloodletting that shook even this combat veteran to the very depths of his being. (*The Executioner: Nightmare in New York.*)

It was here that he encountered the master plan of *Cosa di tutti Cosa*, or the total domination of American life by underworld interests. In his own unique way, Bolan postponed the realization of that master plan even while accepting the fact that he could never, by himself, totally destroy the Mafia. It was a war of impossible dimensions which one man alone could never hope to win. Thus began the new phase of the Bolan Wars, the *war of frustration*. If he could not cut out the heart of this cancer, he would at least sever an arm here and there, keep them off balance, and keep hacking at them until the world awakened to the reality of this many-tentacled giant bent on devouring it.

Thus also, Chicago. If New York had been a nightmare, then Chicago must surely be the grim awakening, the model city for The Thing of All Things, *Cosa di tutti Cosa*, the Thing already come to pass. For Mack Bolan, Chicago was the inevitable next scene of confrontation with the mob. Certainly he was knowledgeable regarding that triumvirate of power described by bestselling author Ovid Demaris in his masterful work on Chicago, *Captive City:*

"Today it is nearly impossible to differentiate among the partners—the businessman is a politician, the politician is a gangster, and the gangster is a businessman."

So what sort of man is it who single-handedly challenges such a power combine? Is he indeed the same naive soldier who returned from the battlefront of Vietnam to bury his own beloved dead—and then to

16

avenge their deaths? Could *any* sensitive and normally intelligent man undergo the gory violence and continual jeopardy of the Bolan Wars without also undergoing a radical alteration to his personality? It would seem not. Bolan had been growing into his own destiny—certainly into a deeper understanding of the dimensions of his conflict—and most probably into a finer appreciation of the *reasons* for this war.

Shortly before his entry into Chicago, he penned this thought in his personal journal: ". . . it's going to be a wipe-out . . . them or me. I have lost the ability to judge the value of all this. But I'm convinced that it matters, somewhere, which side wins. It matters to the universe. I consign my fate to the needs of the universe."

A man's character *is* his fate. The same could be said of a city, or of a nation.

But what *sort* of man would willingly and alone walk into *The Chicago Wipe-Out*?

Whatever else he might be, Mack Bolan, The Executioner, *is* that sort of man.

1: THE CHALLENGE

In a matter of seconds, Bolan knew, the Chicago War would be on. The face in his crosshairs was the one he had been patiently awaiting for two hours on this crisp winter afternoon beside Lake Michigan. Faces had come and gone through the hairs of the 20-power, but this was the one he had wanted. Once it might have been handsome, or at least it might have possessed a potential for comeliness. Now it showed the indelible tracings of an inner rot, of power and greed too long unrestrained—a face that had seen death and brutality and atrocity far too many times to remain comely in the mirror of humanity—and, yes, this was a face to launch the War for Chicago.

For a second *The Executioner* hesitated. Some deep uneasiness over this hit was gnawing for a quick mental review of the situation. Two days of patient and cautious recon had failed to produce any intelligence which would dissuade him from making the strike at this particular time and place. The big lakeshore estate was reasonably secluded. There was no evidence of a hardset defense—the staff of this Mafia *joint* appeared both modest and relaxed—a small force of hardmen. Bolan had counted only four identifiable gunbearers—one at the gate in front, one acting as a doorman, the other two alternating on relief. The inside crew was made up of a cook, a bartender and a waiter. The guests seemed to bring their female companions with them; there was no *whore-corps* in residence. The two-story joint had six bedrooms on the upper level. The lower level was taken over by the kitchen and dining room, lounge, game room, and a large library that probably served as a conference room.

Bolan could find no reason for his uneasiness. His own position had been carefully selected and was as good a drop as he could reasonably expect to find. He was comfortably situated in the garage apartment of an adjoining estate which had been closed for the winter. He had the wind at his back and a bird's-eye, unrestricted view of the target area. His line of withdrawal provided several acceptable alternate routes of retreat, and he would be firing along a three hundred-meter range—well beyond any effective retort from handguns.

So why the uneasiness? Simple fear, maybe. Or an instinctive recognition of . . . what? Bolan shook away the feeling. The flash review had crowded his mind for only an instant and the long-awaited image of evil was still crowding the vision field of the sniperscope. The target was standing beside the vehicle from which he had just emerged, his face thrust aggressively into the raw wind slanting in from the lake, and he was evidently giving some instructions to his driver. His woman had already gone inside—a luscious blonde in a fur coat who displayed a wiggle that promised everything.

The intense magnification of these big scopes created a distortion of reality; Aurielli's face seemed to be just hanging there—discarnate, a blob of humanity that had somehow managed to insinuate itself in the lens. And, yeah, a war was waiting. Last minute fears or not, the moment had arrived.

Bolan sighed, and his finger knew no compunction as it caressed the trigger of the big Weatherby. The high-powered rifle thundered into the recoil as the .460 Magnum missile tore along the one-second course. Bolan grimaced and rode the recoil, his eye flaring into the scope in the effort to maintain target continuity as the image disintegrated in a frothy implosion of blood and bone and tissue—and Louis Aurielli, Mafia underboss, suddenly ceased to exist in the space-time world.

The bolt-action moved swiftly and smoothly as the Weatherby immediately swung a few degrees left and the long barrel elevated an inch or two to acquire the next target. The dumbly-dismayed visage of Aurielli's pretty-boy bodyguard, one Adonis Sallavecci, hung there for a frozen instant in the framework of doom as it contemplated the inexplicable behavior of a disintegrating boss. The sound-wave bearing the rustling report of that first round reached the target area at about the same instant that the second Magnum mushroomed into Sallavecci's once-pretty face, and another target was fragmented and flung beyond the vision field of the sniperscope.

Again the bolt-action ejected searing metal and the trained eye of the marksman rode the jolting weapon to the next preselected step of the rapid-fire triple punch, and again the tightening finger of death dispatched an emissary of war. As swiftly as three ticks of a clock, three victims of sudden death lay crumpled in the drive of the lakeshore estate that corruption had built.

Aurielli's Cadillac lurched forward, moving head-on toward Bolan's distant position—a purely instinctive reaction of flight. The Weatherby sent it careening out of control on an instantly deflated front tire, then Bolan swung the scope aside for a broader view of the developments down there. His unencumbered eye caught a glint of something in motion at a dormer window atop the joint—the window raised and a figure leaned out to shout something at the hardman at the door, and the upstairs man was pointing in Bolan's general direction. At that same moment he saw a flash from another gable window and instinctively dropped to the floor a split-second before a projectile tore away his own window-facing. Two others came in quick sucession, heavy sizzlers that sent showers of rotting wood flying through the garage apartment.

And Bolan knew now why the uneasy feeling. His recon had not been good enough. The joint *was* a hardsite; they had defenses there that not even a two-day watch had revealed . . . and these Chicago clowns were no clowns—their response had been instantaneous and effective. The reports of several high-powered rifles were blending in a concerted and rapid return fire; they were concentrating on the window areas, keeping Bolan down and ducking while their comrades on the ground below found cover. Heavy calibre slugs were tearing into the building with ominous thumps and the sounds of splintering wood.

Okay, so Bolan knew that game too. They were working a bracketing pattern, intent on keeping him down and clear of those windows. He grimaced and snaked along the floor toward the door, the opening of which was set at a right angle to the line of fire. He lay in the doorway and sent three quick rounds into the grounded Cadillac, then immediately rolled back to his

22

original gunport at the window, smiling with grim satisfaction as the doorjamb began to splinter under the same ferocious counterattack previously accorded the window areas. Three seconds was all Bolan desired . . . three seconds of diverted fire. He could see the flashes from two weapons on the roof across the way and just below these, a weapon at each of the dormer windows. Make it *four* seconds.

The sniperscope was back in place and he was scanning the ridges of the roof. A target came into sharp focus, a face in dark concentration as it fought the rapid recoils of a semi-automatic rifle. Bolan squeezed off a shot and moved the scan onward, allowing no time to verify the hit, smoothly working the bolt-action and immediately acquiring another target, squeezing-off and moving on to the dormers.

The desired four seconds were not forthcoming; his opponents at the windows had already become aware of the maneuver and were retargeting. The shadow of a man in a face-on confrontation appeared in the vision-field, a scope-mounted semi-automatic fore-grounded and spitting flame. Something thwacked into the wood beside Bolan's head as he cooly squeezed off, then rode the recoil into the next target and again sighed into the pull; this target he hung into and watched as it was punched backwards into the distant room. Then he backtracked in a verification of the first three hits, realizing already that this phase of the firefight had ended. A warm trickle of blood was oozing down his cheek. He wiped it away and withdrew the splinter of wood that was producing it, realizing also that he had been *that* close to death.

In a delayed reaction to the doorway fusillade, the

23

Cadillac suddenly erupted into flames with a whooshing explosion that lifted the rear end and resettled the heavy vehicle at an angle to the drive.

People were running about down there, amongst the trees, and someone was shouting instructions. A moment later a lone figure appeared through the hedgerow separating the two properties. He was a dark, thickset man with a Thompson chopper, and Bolan did not need the scope to read the ferocity on that scowling face. Their gazes met in simultaneous discovery and the Thompson began its upward swing. Bolan had to rise to his feet to get the proper depression for the Weatherby; he did so, firing from the hip in the same smooth motion, and the beginning gutteral chop of the Thompson was instantly eclipsed by the rolling *cra-ack* of the Weatherby.

The guy staggered backwards into the hedgerow and was momentarily supported there by the thick bushes, the now silent weapon hugged to his chest and turning crimson, then he toppled forward in a crumbling fall. The excited voice of a man somewhere in the background of action cried, "Christ, he got Blackie!"

Bolan placed a marksman's medal on the shattered windowsill, then whirled and ran for the door. No . . . these were definitely not clowns. The Executioner was beginning to feel like the largest clown of all for walking into a hardset like this one. The enemy was present in force and knew how to respond to a hit. The question now uppermost in Bolan's mind concerned his ability to successfully withdraw. He slung the Weatherby from his shoulder and hit the doorway at full gallop, flinging himself through and over the metal railing of the small porch to drop in a plummeting arc to the frozen ground below, a descent of some fifteen feet. He landed in a shock-absorbing crouch and continued the motion with a rebound toward the protection of the building.

His Beretta was clear of its leather and filling his hand as he rounded the corner of the garage and made a run for the hedgerow. When confronting a superior force, Bolan had learned that confusion and the unexpected were the best equalizers. They would be expecting him to flee; therefore he must charge.

Charge, hell, I'm just retreating to the front!

His maneuver caught three of the enemy in flatfooted indecision as he descended upon them along the hedgerow, the Beretta coughing its chilling little message of defiance. The return fire was disorganized, ineffective, and very brief as two of the *Mafiosi* went down under the assault. The third, a skinny youth with mottled skin and very frightened eyes, stood quietly staring into the full extension of the black Beretta, his mouth open and his own weapon dangling impotently toward the ground. The gunhand was rapidly turning red under a flow of blood from a shoulder wound. The gunner's eyes flicked briefly from the bore of the Beretta to the icy gaze of *The Executioner,* then skittered away to fasten on the dead man lying at his feet.

Coldly, Bolan asked him, "You ready to die, soldier?"

The gunner shook his head in a negative response and the revolver slipped from his hand.

"How many more of you?" Bolan demanded.

"Just me," the youth mumbled. His gaze once more raised to Bolan's cool inspection, then again fell. "And I'm hit," he added dully.

Bolan said, "Count your blessings." He tossed a

25

marksman's medal toward the defeated man's feet. "Pick it up," he commanded. "See that Lavallo gets it. Tell him he's next."

The *Mafioso* scooped up the medal with his good hand. He inspected it with suddenly expressive eyes and said, "Hell, I guessed it. I figured it must be you. Jeezus, Bolan, I—"

The Executioner's graveyard voice commanded, "Take off."

The guy took off, staggering back through the hedgerow without a backwards glance, and undoubtedly counting his blessings.

Bolan stepped over a dead body and strode quickly toward the garage and his waiting vehicle. The mob, he was thinking, would not overlook a challenge like that.

The die was cast.

The Chicago Wipe-Out was on.

And maybe something else was on, as well. The mind-blowing blonde with the million-dollar wiggle, whom Bolan had last seen entering the hardsite, was standing beside his Ferrari and breathing hard as she agitatedly watched his approach. Her hair was in a wild tangle, and somewhere she'd become parted from the fur coat—a loss she could hardly afford, considering the costume she had left. The girl was practically naked, and Bolan couldn't decide if she was shivering from the cold or from terror. Either way, something else was definitely on.

2: A FOXY LADY

"I'm on your s-side. Take me with you. *Please!*"

If she'd looked good in the sniperscope, she was downright edible in the three-dimensional reality as she moved jerkily around to Bolan's side of the car. A tall girl, pushing close to the six-foot mark, but put together in eye-gathering proportions, with those softly alluring contours that are sometimes seen on a budding ballerina who has not yet gone to solid muscle.

The costume would have been a bit much for the classical ballet crowd, though. It was made of red fur, a one-piece bit of fluff with a microscopic bottom that was hardly more than a G-string, and a thin strip stretching up each side to loop about into a decorative but entirely non-concealing swirl across luxurious breastworks. A bushy red tail reaching to her knees completed the picture—except for the head of a leering fox, done in bodypaint and peering out from the soft valley between her breasts.

Discounting the tail, Bolan figured he could hide the costume in his hand. The only other items of apparel were soft, ankle-high moccasins—and the temperature was in the mid-thirties with a stiff breeze raking in from the lake. It was no time to be recruiting a women's auxiliary—but it was also no time for any human being to be prancing about the shores of Lake Michigan in a bedroom combat suit. And she was about to cave in completely—swaying like a reed in the wind fighting to get her breathing and her emotions under control, all the while turning a deeper shade of blue. Bolan silently stowed the Weatherby and debated the question of what to do about the girl. Finally he gave her a reluctant okay with his eyes and she tumbled into the car with a shivery moan of thanks—it was not entirely certain whether she was thanking Bolan or a higher power.

He slid in beside her, snared his topcoat from the rear deck and draped it over her. Silently she bundled herself in it and drew the long, sculpted legs into the seat to cover them also, then went into a chattering case of the shakes.

The girl was still shivering when the Ferrari cleared the scene and took up a casual southward cruise along Lake Shore Drive. Bolan was in no great hurry now. He produced a quart thermos and poured his passenger a slug of steaming coffee. She accepted it with a grateful sweep of the eyes and quickly began to settle down.

When the coffee was nearly consumed Bolan lit a cigarette and handed it to her along with his first words. "You're looking better," he growled.

"Thanks," she said in an unsteady voice. "Feeling better."

A police car with beacon flashing tore past on a northward track, weaving through the traffic on a hot call to Bolan guessed where—and followed closely by a second and then a third. His guest was huddled in the topcoat and working hard at the cigarette, exhaling with

28

audible tremors, but she had also noted the passage of the police. She wriggled about on the seat and murmured, "Thanks for getting me away from there."

He grunted and tried the heater, found it mildly warm, and told her, "Out of the frying pan and into the fire."

"What?"

"That's you. You picked a hard taxi, lady."

She raked him with sky blue eyes and made a stab at a smile. "I know," she said. "You're Mack Bolan, aren't you?"

"Stretch your feet to the heater," he commanded gruffly.

She did so, carefully arranging the coat to capture the warmth. Then her gaze became fixed on Bolan's profile and he felt it quietly absorbing him. Presently she announced, "I'm a Foxy Lady."

Bolan gave her his full attention for a moment, inspecting her with a sober gaze. He pegged her age in the low twenties. The eyes were luminous and intelligent; under different conditions she would be a girl who laughed easily. Maybe she would be capable of warmth and sincerity. She returned his stare, and nothing more—no invitation, no challenge, no bid for sympathy—simply a frank return of interest.

Bolan showed her half a smile and told her, "Yeah, you're pretty foxy."

She said, "No, I mean—"

"I know what you mean," he assured her. Bolan had not been *that* much out of things. The Foxy Ladies had become an international trademark of female sensuality, standard-bearers of *Foxy Magazine* and the widely popular *Lair* keyclubs. The technically nude young beauties were the symbols of a farflung male-oriented business empire—and to become a Foxy Lady was an almost certain threshold to bigger and better things for aspiring models and actresses. Sure, Bolan and several million other Vietnam veterans knew about the Foxy Ladies. Their centerfold artwork had adorned every barracks, tent and vehicle in Southeast Asia.

This one had bent toward the ashtray to crush out the cigarette. The topcoat fell away from her. She sighed and let it remain where it fell. The limited airspace of the Ferrari cabin was beginning to heat up. She neatly folded the coat and arranged it over the backrest. Then she repositioned herself to face Bolan and drew one leg onto the seat. Bolan cooly inspected the display of living flesh, then directed his eyes to the business of piloting the vehicle.

"What you see is what you don't get," she told him in a matter-of-fact tone, paraphrasing a famous black comedian. "That's the house rule at the *Lair*. It's an exercise in male frustration, I guess."

"What are the house rules for Mafia molls?" he quietly inquired.

The blue eyes flared but the reply was just as quiet. "Believe it or not, this was my first time at that place. I knew what Mr. Aurielli was, of course. But you have to understand . . . in this town, that's almost a mark of distinction. There was nothing personal between us. I'd just met him this afternoon."

Bolan was watching for roadsigns, trying to orient himself. Almost absently, he commented, "Okay."

"It was an assignment," she explained. "It's in our contract. We get outside assignments. Not uh . . . not what you might be thinking."

"Uh huh."

"It's a public relations thing. The Foxy Ladies often make appearances at private parties. It's good for us, or so we're told. We get more exposure that way." Her eyes flashed down to the costume. "If that's possible."

Bolan said, "Okay."

"Do you want to hear this or don't you?"

"I'm listening," he assured her. He was also trying to find his place on a map of the city.

"Mr. Aurielli is—*was*—a keyholder. Do you think I'd go on a date dressed like this? In the middle of the afternoon? I was out there to serve a special meeting. Mr. Aurielli called it a board meeting. But I didn't see any other board members present, and I was already beginning to smell a rat when the shooting started. This man, the bartender I guess, had just taken my coat and was headed off somewhere to put it away. When the first shot sounded, he ran toward the back of the house. I went to the window, and by that time the shots were coming one after another and I saw Mr. Aurielli and two other men lying in the drive. I guess I panicked. I ran outside . . . and then I saw the men upstairs shooting at the place next door. Then the car caught fire and blew up. I heard someone yell something about *Bolan*—and that's when I started running. I don't know why I ran to you. I guess I just suddenly realized where I needed to be."

Bolan glanced at her and caught a wry smile pulling at her lips. "My suspicious and romantic mind, I guess," she continued. "I had suddenly understood that I was practically alone with that . . . that terrible man—and in some sort of a hideout. So I had already begun to panic. And I guess I thought Prince Charming had come to

31

rescue me from my awful fate. I don't know what I thought. I just lost my head. And I ran for the arms of Prince Charming."

"And found him to be no prince," Bolan commented dryly.

"You carried me away in your white charger, didn't you," she quietly observed.

"Call it a white coffin," he suggested. "That's what it could turn into."

"I guess I knew what I was doing," the girl murmured. "We—the girls at the club—we were talking about you just the other night. They had that special from New York on Channel 4, and we were talking about your—uh—battles there. Someone said you'd never come to Chicago. The people around here are kind of crazy—or have you noticed that? They seem to be proud to be the crime center of the universe. Anyway, I suppose all this was in my mind—and the shooting started—and I heard that man on the roof shout your name. I guess I knew where I was running. Still I guess I didn't know for sure until I saw you walking toward the car in that black suit. Then it all came together. The Executioner *had* come to Chicago."

Bolan said, "And right in the nick of time, eh?"

"I guess that's how I thought of it," she admitted. "Very egotistic, huh. Just the same, you *did* save my life back there, you know."

"Not quite," he told her.

"What?"

"Look, I believe your story," he said. "I could just as easily disbelieve it, but I *have* to lean your way. And you have to lean with me. Now you think carefully and answer the same way. How many people knew you were

32

going to that joint with Aurielli?"

She blinked her eyes rapidly and replied, "Lots of people. It was an assignment. I told you. I was sent—"

"Okay. Now what do you suppose is going to happen when the mob begins looking into the thing? They're going to discover there's a chick missing from the woodpile. They're going to wonder what happened to the chick and they're going to wonder if there was any connection between her and Bolan. These guys don't miss any bets. They're as good as any cops anywhere when it comes to pulling evidence together. They know their business, and they conduct it with a notable absence of tenderness. Sooner or later they're going to start wondering about a certain Foxy Lady. And if they develop any suspicion whatever that maybe this lady helped set up that little slaughter out there this afternoon, then that lady will be not very long for this world. Are you leaning with me?"

She was. Bolan had to believe that the reaction was genuine. Her eyes fluttered, the veneer of sophistication cracked a bit further, and she exclaimed, "Oh wow! That's what you meant by 'out of the frying pan and into the fire.' "

Bolan assured her, "That's exactly what I meant."

"So what do I do now?" she asked in a small voice. "Go back?"

He shook his head. "It's too late for that. The cops are already swarming the joint. No, you have to go on. But we have to build you a story. You panicked and ran. A guy picked you up and took you into town. You . . ." The look in her eyes stopped him. He asked, "What's wrong?"

"It's no good," she replied miserably. "They saw me.

33

Two men. I saw them watching me from the kitchen window as I was running. They had to know where I was headed."

Bolan said, "Well damn it."

"I guess you could take me to a police station," she suggested in a frightened voice. "I could ask for protection."

He shook his head. "That wouldn't buy you a thing. Not if these people decide to get to you."

"Then take me home," she said, suddenly flaring with defiance. "I live in Elmhurst. I'll call the club and tell them what happened, and I'll just go on as though nothing had happened. If the mobsters come to me, I'll just tell them exactly how it was. And they can like it or lump it."

Bolan was obviously neither liking nor lumping it. His face was etched with trouble lines, and again he said, "Well damn it."

Perhaps he was remembering the gruesome remains of what had been an equally beautiful and innocent girl, left behind in a New York morgue; or maybe he was thinking of an exotic French actress who had offered him Eden on the Riviera and who had found in return nothing but an echo of Bolan's hell—or a valiant little Cuban exile who had given her blood for his in Miami and died in agony with a blowtorch at her breasts. And perhaps he was viewing the entire procession of beloved dead.

He turned tortured eyes to the latest most likely candidate and told her, "Like it or not, Foxy, you're a part of my jungle now."

It was all Bolan needed to make his job doubly impossible . . . another defenseless ally to worry over. He jerked the wheel viciously into the exit to an east-west arterial and left Lake Shore Drive behind. He had found his orientation.

This new development called for a change in the battle order.

And Bolan knew precisely what had to be done next.

3: THE DEAL

"For God's sake, Pete, where you been? I been looking all over for you!"

The king of the highways, Pietro D. (Pete the Hauler) Lavallo regarded his "Executive Vice-President" with a superior smugness and a condescending smile. "While you been running around looking for me," he replied, "I been out nailing down a deal." He went on to his desk and dropped, tiredly, into a massive chair. "So what's your problem, Rudy? What're you so lathered-up about, huh?"

Rudy Palmer (*nee* Colombo Palmeiri) was swaying nervously from one foot to the other. His eyes went to the wall behind his boss's head as he said, "I don't know just how to tell you this, Pete. I got some bad news."

"Well just tell it and let me figure out how bad it is, huh, Rudy?"

"Louis Aurielli is dead."

"Did you say *dead*?"

"Yeah. He's dead, Pete."

Pete the Hauler's eyes shaded into a dull gaze while the message tried to locate a level of acceptance in the gray matter behind those eyes. Disbelief registered there even as he was replying, "Hell, I *warned* him. I *told* him those pains were trying t' tell him something. You mean

37

he's really *dead?*" He snapped his fingers. "Just like *that?*"

"No!" Palmer exclaimed. "Not like that. I mean his brains are splattered all over Lakeside. Him and about a dozen boys. City Jim says bodies are strung all around the joint, just shot to hell."

Lavallo slowly pushed his swivel chair away from the desk and eased to his feet. As if in a slow-motion reflex he opened a drawer and picked up a .45 Colt autoloader, checked the clip, and placed it on the desk. Then he went to the window and stared out upon the warehouse complex that surrounded the modernistic office building. In a barely audible voice he asked, "And where does City Jim come into it?"

"Hell, I guess they got half the police force out there, that's where he comes into it. He said to tell you—"

"*He* said?" Lavallo snarled, whirling away from the window. "You mean he called personal?"

"Yes he did, and let me tell you about it, Pete." Palmer took time to light a cigarette, exhaling with the burst of words. "You remember a Lakeside soldier called Johnny Vegas? Tall skinny kid, always doing card tricks?"

Lavallo cried, "Get to it! What the hell happened out there?"

"This Johnny Vegas is the only soldier left alive up there. He says it was a *Bolan* hit. He says he stood eye-to-eye with the bastard and—"

Lavallo had scooped up an ashtray from the desk and thrown it the length of the office. It struck the far wall and shattered, dislodging a heavy plaque.

Palmer yelled, "Calm down, Pete! God, listen to what I got to tell you!"

"Awright I'm listening." Lavallo picked up the .45

38

and thrust it into the waistband of his trousers. "I'm *listening*! Go ahead!"

"Johnny Vegas says Bolan left a message for you. That's why City Jim called direct. He says you better take a vacation, and damn quick. Bolan gave the kid one of those medals—you know, those calling-cards of his. He said Johnny should give it to you, because you're next."

Lavallo's eyes twitched. He muttered, "Smart son of a bitch. Where the hell does he get off with—just who the hell does he think he is?"

"Who? You mean City Jim? He's just trying—"

"Hell no, I mean that smart bastard!" Lavallo yelled. "Where the hell does he think he's at, still in New York or somewheres? He can't pull that stuff in this town, don't he know that?"

"God, I guess he already pulled it, Pete," Rudy Palmer quietly pointed out. "The guy's a nut, you know that. You can't figure a nut. He's probably all horsed up, you know how those guys come back from Vietnam. Popping four or five caps of horse a day and clear outta their skulls with the stuff. I think you ought to—"

"Aw shut up," Lavallo muttered. "Lemme think. Hell I ain't even got used to Lou being dead yet. Lemme think."

"Well listen to one more thing first. I already sent for Nicko and Eddie. I told them to round up plenty of soldiers and get a convoy out here to take you home. I don't want you taking no chances with this nut."

"Yeah, yeah—okay." Lavallo was staring at the window, his eyes glazed and unseeing. "And tell City Jim thanks if he calls back. Tell him I appreciate the personal interest."

Palmer nodded and went to the door, then turned

39

back to examine his boss with a searching gaze. "There was a doll with Louis when he got it," he announced quietly.

"It figures," Lavallo muttered.

"And she up and disappeared. The chef says he saw her running across the grounds to meet Bolan. He says she knew right where she was going."

Lavallo's chin quivered. He said, "I told Lou those dollies would kill him. A man fifty-five years old shouldn't try acting like a young stud again. I warned him those pains meant something."

"The point is that—"

"I know what point it is!" Lavallo yelled.

"Well I'm going to put a crew working that angle."

"You do that, Rudy. And tell 'em to bring this doll to me. I want to talk to her personal."

"I figured you would," Rudy Palmer replied, and went on out, carefully closing the door between the interconnecting offices.

Lavallo absently patted the grip of the .45 and sank onto the corner of the desk, still staring unseeingly at the window. Shock and anger and fear and outrage all seemed to have become resolved in a consummate sadness. Louis Aurielli had been a good friend, a lifelong companion. They had come up together, through the bloody ranks of family competition to a plateau of unchallenged power. They'd seen a lot together, and done a lot together—and together they had become a lot. Now Lavallo felt strangely alone, exposed to the vicissitudes of a cruel world. And because of what? Because of a smart-ass soldier boy on a dumb vendetta. What had Louis Aurielli known of this smart-ass? What did Pete Lavallo care about him?

Okay, sure, there had been that thing at Miami

Beach. And some of the Chicago boys caught hell at Miami. But Lou and Pete had been a hundred miles away at the time, and why should they take it personal about Miami Beach? Let the street soldiers worry about the blacksuited bastard, that's what they were paid to do. Not Lou and Pete. But now here was Louis dead and Pete worrying.

There just wasn't any justice.

Well . . . it was personal now for Pete Lavallo. People didn't go around gunning down his lifelong friends and live to smile about it. Not nobody, not Mack Bolan, not a hundred Mack Bolans.

Lavallo sat there for a long time . . . remembering, wondering, hating . . . and then he realized that the sun had gone down and that it was getting dark outside. He went to the window and pulled the blind, then turned on his desk lamp and punched an intercom button to connect him with a desk situated deep in the maze of warehouses. A nervous voice responded immediately and Lavallo asked it, "Did that guy from Rockford show up yet?"

"Not yet, Mr. Lavallo," came the strained response.

"Who the hell does he think he is?" Lavallo snarled. "I told him four o'clock, and here it is five."

"They were having an ice storm across Interstate 90, sir, up near Belvidere. Possibly he got caught in that."

"Don't bullshit me no ice storms!" Lavallo raged. "When he gets in, if he ever gets in, you tell him it's all off. Tell him he's not hauling for Lavallo and Aurielli, not if he can't show up on time for the first haul!"

The choked voice replied, "He's leased fifty trucks for that job, Mr. Lavallo. I don't believe we could just arbitrarily terminate his contract, especially if an act of God is the cause of his delay."

41

"Arbitrary, who the hell said anything about arbitrary? You tell that guy the contract is tore up, and if he wants an act of God, ask him what he thinks about a spanner wrench against the side of the head. I ain't holding still for no smart-ass out-of-town hauler that thinks he can walk all over L & A. And the same goes for a smart-ass dispatcher that talks about arbitrary stuff. Don't you forget that."

"Yes sir. I'll tell him to run his fifty leased trucks up his ass, Mr. Lavallo."

"You do that!" Lavallo punched off the connection and settled into his chair, puffing with anger.

The side door opened and Rudy Palmer stood there stiffly framed in the rectangle of light. "The convoy is downstairs, Pete," he announced quietly. "Let's go home."

"Go on down," Lavallo said. "I gotta take a piss, then I'll be right with you. Did anybody tell Mrs. Aurielli about Louis?"

"We're trying to locate her," Palmer replied woodenly. "She's usually in Nassau this time of year."

"If you don't find her there, try that hotel at St. Thomas. She likes it there, too. Go on, Rudy. I'll be right down."

Palmer backed out and closed the door. Lavallo smiled wryly to himself and picked up the telephone. A moment later he got his connection and told it, "Hello, John? This is Pete Lavallo. You know, L & A Trucking. Say, uh, one of my subcontractors has crapped out on me. You know what I was saying last week about something big for your campaign fund."

A clipped voice rattled back a brisk response.

Lavallo grinned and said, "Yeah, well that was a drop in the bucket, I don't even count that. I meant something *big*. That, uh, kid of yours—John Junior, is it? Listen, I know where he can pick up long-term leases on fifty heavy haulers at a fraction of the regular cost."

A delighted response rattled the receiver.

The Lavallo grin widened. He said, "Sure, it's the cheapest way I know to get into the trucking business. Listen, you send John Junior around in the morning, eh? We'll see what we can come up with."

Another rattle, then: "Oh, hell, don't mention it, John. What are friends for if they can't look out for each other, eh?"

Lavallo hung up and studied his fingertips with a smug smile. One man's ruin always meant another man's gain. And what the hell could the punk from Rockford possibly mean to Pete Lavallo?

He got into his overcoat and again checked the load in the .45 and dropped it into a coat pocket, took a quick look about the office, and went out. He thought again of Aurielli and knew that he would not accept the fact of Lou's death until he saw him lying there in his coffin, all done up for planting. Meanwhile life had to go on. Business details had to be kept tidy. He touched the grip of the .45—and yeah, life had to go on.

Quickly he descended the stairway. The small office building was quiet and deserted. It mildly irked Lavallo the way the hired help all got up and ran out at the stroke of five. It would seem like they would take more interest in the business. After all, it was their bread and butter, wasn't it? Maybe he'd shake up this goddam crew, get them on their toes, and either shape 'em up or ship 'em out. That idea appealed to him, and he continued on toward the lobby in a rising good humor.

The news about Louis had really shaken him. He was glad to be pulling out of that dark mood. His ulcers got

43

edgy when *he* got edgy, and he sure didn't want a flareup of *them* goddam things.

Rudy Palmer was seated on the bottom step—waiting for the boss—tying his shoe or something. The good humor deepened. Rudy might not be overly bright, especially in business matters, but he could be a comfort to a guy. Imagine him saying that this Bolan was horsed up! Lavallo experienced an unbidden tremor. If only it were true. It was, of course, not true. Mack the Bastard Bolan was the most scarey damn thing to come up in all of Lavallo's experiences. You couldn't explain away a guy like that as a *junkie*, for God's sake. And now the bastard was in Chicago. And there sat Rudy, one of the best gunners in the business, hovering at the bottom of the steps and waiting patiently for the boss, plus a whole crew of gun soldiers waiting outside to escort the boss safely home. So why the hell should Pete Lavallo be worried at all?

He brushed past Palmer with a gruff, "Let's go, let's go," and got halfway to the door before realizing that Rudy was not following him. He turned back and said, "Hey! You sleeping on the job?"

Then Lavallo noted the dark discoloration on the carpet immediately in front of Rudy Palmer, and he realized that Rudy was sitting in one hell of an awkward position. He hurried back to the stairway and grabbed Palmer's shoulder and shook it. The whole torso wobbled and the head flopped limply back to reveal a gaping slit across the throat, wide-open eyes stared blankly at the ceiling for a moment, then Rudy Palmer's remains toppled over.

Lavallo recoiled and danced clear of the falling body. His hand was fumbling for his coat pocket and the comforting grip of the .45 and he was making a run for

44

the door before he was even aware of his actions.

It was then that the tall man in the black suit stepped from the shadows near the door, a long silencer-tipped black blaster targeted on Pete the Hauler's head, tight lips pulled back in a killer snarl to reveal gleaming teeth. Again Lavallo recoiled and came to an abrupt halt, but his hand continued to dig for the .45.

Two quick spurts of flame arced away from the black blaster—accompanied by quiet phutting sounds—and something hot and furious tore through the fabric of Lavallo's overcoat. His hand came out of there quickly, a double furrow plowed across the top of it.

Two words, about as clipped and final as the phuts from the silencer, were spat at him. "Freeze, Lavallo."

Pete the Hauler froze, but his stomach did not. The ulcers were already yelling bloody murder when Lavallo coughed nervously and asked, "Bolan? Is that Mack Bolan?"

"Did you get my message from Lakeside, Lavallo?"

"I got it. Sure I got it. And here's one for you. There's a whole gun crew waiting just outside that door. They can see you clear as anything, Bolan. They're looking at you right now."

"You're dreaming, Lavallo," the icy voice informed him.

Pete the Hauler shivered and stole a glance through the plate-glass of the lobby. There was no sign of any cars waiting out there. He said, "Look, Bolan, I got nothing—"

"That's right, you've got nothing. Rudy sent your gunners home. It's just you and me, Lavallo. Now you take off the overcoat and let it fall to the floor. Then you kick it away."

Lavallo followed the instructions. Those bastard eyes

were tearing him up. Inwardly he was raging and his stomach was throwing fits. Outwardly he was smooth, almost genial. He told his persecutor, "If you were going to kill me, you'd have done it already. So what's going on, Bolan?"

"I've got a girl," the man in black said tightly. "I mean to keep her alive. And *well*. You remember that. She's your personal responsibility. Whatever happens to her happens also to you, Lavallo. Remember that. She gets cut a little, I cut you a little. She gets burned a little, I burn you a little. She gets left alone, you get left alone. Call that a deal, with no escape clause. You're tied to her, Lavallo, in life and in death. Remember it."

The king of the highways nervously wet his lips and said, "You're talking about the dollie was with Lou. Louis Aurielli."

"That's the one. She just stumbled into this thing, Pietro. It was a dumb mistake. See that it stays that way. Now turn around and go back up the stairs."

"I don't get it!" Lavallo cried, the rage finally surfacing and shaking him. "You'd trade *me* for one little chippie?"

"It's bargain basement day," Bolan told him. "Usually the price would be one of her for a hundred of your kind. Now get on up the stairs before I decide to deal with bigger fish."

Lavallo turned and got. He pounded up the stairs and paused at the landing to inspect the bullet grazes on his hand and to attempt to quell the tumbling of his guts, then he staggered on toward the office.

Maybe Rudy had been right after all, he was thinking. God, didn't that big dumb bastard know he couldn't pull that kind of stuff in this town? Did he think this was New York or Miami or somewheres? Did he think he could just walk in and take over *Chicago?*

Lavallo hurried past his own doorway and pushed into Palmer's office. *City Jim,* that was the one to call. These goddam punk cops had to get their heads out of their asses and nail that goddam guy.

He fell into Palmer's swivel chair and began hastily going through the scattered papers on the desk. Who the hell did Rudy call? What crew did he put on that dollie? *Call City Jim,* that was the thing to do. First, though; first he had to find that crew and call them off. Did that bastard say *tied* in *life* and *death?*

Lavallo shivered violently and intensified his investigation of Rudy's desk. God, he didn't want to be tied to no *turkey.* God no. Not until that horsed-up, blacksuited dummy was out of the way. Lavallo had to believe that guy. He'd do it. He'd do just what he promised he'd do.

He'd better get in touch with the council, though. He'd better talk it over with the bosses. But *should* he? *Could* he keep them out of it? Hell, he had to, he *had* to. They'd probably say, "Bring *us* that dollie, Pete the Hauler, and let *us* decide what she's worth."

The king of the highways lurched to his feet and made a dash for the toilet, both hands clapped across his mouth. Them goddam ulcers. That goddam Bolan. Fuckin' no good sluts playin' around with older men. Why'd they have to . . . ?

He made it to the basin just in time, and there disgorged an untenable collection of rage and sorrow and greed and fear—especially fear.

Pietro Lavallo had no ulcers.

He was suffering from inner rot.

4: STORM SIGNALS

As night draped itself across the huge city beside the lake, two major storms also appeared to be in imminent descension. One was approaching from the northwest, in the form of snow and high winds and plummeting temperatures. The other was materializing within the city itself, and took the form of worried officials, bustling police movements, and multitudinous stirrings in diverse places.

The lights at City Hall continued to burn brightly into the night, specifically in and about the offices of the mayor and commissioner of police. Standard riot forces were ordered to duty *in civilian clothes*, uniformed patrols were beefed up and re-deployed, and special motorized units were stationed at key points.

Never a city to disregard its own romantic flavors, Chicago's radio disc jockeys that evening interspersed their regular format with funeral dirges dedicated to various fictitious and Runyonesque characters: Sammy Slink, Willie the Weasel, Tommy Torpedo, *et al*—and two local television stations pre-empted network programming to run special "background commentaries" on the life and times of one Mack Bolan.

The Executioner had come to town, and all of Chicago seemed to be aware of his arrival. That other

49

storm, advancing slowly from the north, drew hardly any notice at all—except from the luckless city employees who were ordered into all-night street service.

In a private room above a Michigan Avenue tavern, a small group of quietly sober men were planning a storm of their own. Unofficially referred to as "The Quad Council," these four represented the invisible power structure which had welded the city and its environs into an impregnable stronghold of criminal corruption. Its members were referred to only as *City, Labor, Industry,* and *Syndicate.*

In this meeting were worked out the various lines of responsibility, the "action interfaces," and the dimensions of effort to be thrown into the upcoming war. From this meeting were fielded generals with strange sounding names leading troops with even stranger talents, and a general of all the generals was named to directly oversee the war effort on behalf of the Quad Council.

This lord high enforcer was one Lawrence "Turkey" Rossi—usually known as *Larry Turk* or, simply, *Turk*. The term *Turkey*, in general Mafia parlance, is used in relation to a particularly gruesome method of torture-interrogation or torture-revenge in which the victim is systematically reduced to a mindless mass of mutilated and writhing flesh, or "turkey," though conscious and screaming for mercy right into the moment of death. Its practitioners develop a high degree of skill, and Larry Turk had received his nickname in recognition of his own high development of this delicate art, acquired during his earlier years of advancement along the rungs of power.

This appointment to lead the counter-war against

Bolan represented a new challenge, and perhaps a new pinnacle of achievement, for the ambitions of Lawrence Rossi. Forty-one years of age and a two-time "graduate" of the Illinois State Prison at Joliet, Larry the Turk had arrived at the high moment of a vicious career. And it must have seemed to him that all roads from this point led straight up.

On this night of the storm, however, the turkey-maker was to discover that even the most sublime roads always travel in more than one direction. Even in Chicago.

Bolan let himself into the motel room and deposited his parcels on a table by the door. The room was lighted only by a sliver of illumination from the bathroom door and the glow from a television screen.

The girl was sprawled casually across the bed on her forearms, her attention absorbed by the television set, a bath towel draped carelessly over her bottom. The Foxy Lady costume lay on a luggage rack at the foot of the bed.

Bolan took in the towel-draped highrise and quickly shifted his focus to a less disturbing scene, the murmuring television. His own image was being displayed there as a blown-up artist's sketch while an off-camera voice was giving a resumé of the New York battles.

The blonde head swivelled slowly about and she regarded him quietly across a rose-petal shoulder which was glowing fetchingly in the reflected light from the television screen. The voice was small and maybe a bit weepy as she told him, "I thought you'd deserted. I've been lying here feeling sorry for myself."

"Had to stop and see a guy," Bolan explained.

"Yes, I know." A shadow seemed to move across her

51

eyes. "They just reported the . . . man . . . at the trucking company. They said it's connected to the executions at Lakeside. Is it?"

He said, "Sure," and tossed a flat box onto the bed. "Better check the fit."

She ignored the box. Again that shadow crossed her eyes as she asked, "Did you really slit his throat?"

Bolan shrugged. "Dead is dead," he muttered, and strode into the bathroom. He called back "Get some clothes on," and banged the door shut.

Sure he'd slit the throat, and he'd punched hot metal into a dozen other men this day—beautiful lady. He had noted that look in her eyes, that dawning revulsion—somehow he had never become accustomed to that look. He supposed he never would, no matter how often he saw it. Well, so what?—he had it coming, didn't he? It was a proper reaction.

So too someone had to be the butcher. Bolan could live with it. A guy with a genius for math should not shrink from numbers . . . a dancer should dance, a singer should sing, a painter should paint, and an executioner should. . . . Bolan knew what he had to do. He knew where his talents lay, and let the revulsion fall where it would. He could live with it.

He flung away the entire train of thought and began undressing for the shower. The Beretta and sideleather went on a towel rack just outside the shower stall, and Bolan went in beneath the stinging spray, lifting his face directly into the invigorating assault. He remained there a long time, eyes clenched, breathing through his mouth, luxuriating in the bombardment—and then he became aware that the door to the stall was open and he felt eyes on him.

They were solemnly glowing eyes and they belonged

52

to the Foxy Lady . . . and there were no shadows or veils there now. In her hand was a cosmetic jar and upon that divine body was nothing but the painted likeness of a red fox.

Soberly, she said, "Thanks for remembering the body cream."

His mind traveled the several corners of the world before he replied, "Okay."

"I'll wash your back if you'll cream-off my paint."

He said, "You're on," and pulled her into the stall.

Soft arms went about him and the resilient body-bountiful welded itself to him in a shivery embrace. Her lips nipped at his shoulder and she moaned, "I'm Jimi James, let's get that into the record."

Bolan ran his hands along the luxurious flesh of her back as he told her, "Pleased to meet you, Miss James. I'm still Mack Bolan."

"Oh, and I'm glad, I'm glad," she whispered, and her mouth found his, and Bolan knew that she was glad. And so was he. Revulsion he could live with, sure—but this was something to live *for*.

If revulsion had indeed been present some moments earlier, it had certainly given way now to something more moving than violence, more jarring than a chunk of muzzle-heated metal, and infinitely more sublime than unending warfare. A man and a woman had found an exalted bond that surpasses all human definitions. And as the storm forces gathered about and above the landscapes surrounding them, there was engendered between them and by them a storm of an entirely different sort . . .

The sign on the specially constructed door read *Communications, Ltd.*—inside were rows of semi-enclosed tables, each equipped with a telephone and other devices helpful to the bookmaker's trade. This was the headquarters of a wire-betting service, a national operation covering race tracks and sporting events throughout the country. Tonight it was covering a different type of event; this was the Chicago nerve center for the War against Bolan. Several dozen men manned the telephones, displayed information, and passed along reports and instructions pertinent to the task at hand.

Larry Turk was holding court with several of his crew chiefs in a turret of desks and wirecages at the rear when someone observed, "Here comes Pete the Hauler."

Turk muttered, "What the hell does that guy want to be . . . ?" He jammed a cigar into his mouth and lit it while the portly underboss made his way along the line of wiremen.

Lavallo was puffing slightly as he rounded the corner into the turret. He gave a little hand signal and said, "Hi Turk. How's it going?"

"Fine, just fine, Mr. Lavallo. What can we do for you?" This was polite notice that the *Caporegime* was neither wanted nor needed here.

"I'm just too nervous to sit around and wait," Lavallo admitted. "I thought maybe I could lend a hand."

Turk's eyes went to the ceiling. This was a delicate matter. At the moment, he was kingpin. Tomorrow, or next week, one day soon, Pete Lavallo's great rank could squash a dozen Larry Turks into nothingness. He told the underboss, "That's great, Mr. Lavallo. Not much happening right now, though. The guy's crawled into a hole somewhere, I guess."

The trucker dropped into a chair. "I'd rather be here than sitting around wondering," he muttered.

Turk exchanged glances with a crew chief. He told Lavallo, "We were just reviewing the strategy. We, uh, got a whole invisible crew tailin' you around, Mr. Lavallo. If you're gonna spend the night here, we need to put those boys someplace else."

Lavallo's eyes showed his surprise. "Nobody told me that," he said.

"No sir, nobody meant to."

"I got my own damn hardmen," the *Caporegime* huffed.

"Yes sir, that's the idea. A double line. One obvious, one not—not even to you."

Lavallo lost the clash of eyes. His went to the floor and he growled, "It's your show, Turk. I, uh, won't be around long. I just dropped in for a look-see. I guess you got things pretty well in hand."

"Thanks. Look, uh, it would be better if you went on natural-like. Bolan tried for you once tonight. We expect he'll try again. We want him to." He slapped his hands together. "Then *pow!* Eh?"

"I get the idea," Lavallo said with a tired smile. "I just ain't exactly used to being a sitting duck, a decoy at that." He struggled to his feet. "Uh, what're you doing, uh, about that dollie?"

Turk shrugged. "The usual things. We got her name, her address, her hangouts. We know where she gets her teeth fixed and who gives her her pelvics. We know her momma and her poppa, and we've had a tap on their phone for over an hour, clear out in Montana. Don't you worry, Mr. Lavallo. When she comes out, we'll know it."

"You don't forget, I got an interest, a right. I wanta know about her and Louis. You don't touch her until I say so."

"My only interest is Bolan. Whatever I have to do to get to Bolan, Mr. Lavallo, I'll have to do. You know that. After that . . ." Turk sighed delicately. ". . . you're welcome to her."

A lineman had hurried into the turret and was anxiously awaiting a chance to break into the conversation. Turk acknowledged his presence with a sliding glance. The man told him, "Chollie Sanders, over at Neighborhood Protective, just gimme something. One of his pigeons, a dress shop on West Washington, called in a suspicious. About an hour late, but they didn't think anything about it until they got home and turned on the television. This guy's wife—"

Turk said impatiently, "Just give me the tip."

"Well this guy come into their shop just as they were closing. Bought a complete outfit for a woman, underwear and everything, gave the old lady the sizes and let her pick everything out." He glanced at Lavallo. "This was just a little while after the hit on L & A."

Turk was giving the man a harsh gaze. Presently he said, "So?"

"So the guy wasn't worrying about prices or styles or anything. He just wanted a complete outfit. And the sizes add up to that Foxy Lady. The guy adds up, too. Tall, kinda dark, wore sunglasses and they didn't get much of a look at his face. But he was dressed all in black, even his overcoat."

Turk grabbed the lineman's elbow and steered him to a large map which was opened across a desk. "Okay," he said quietly. "You just draw a circle where that dress shop is."

The man did so, adding, "Oh, and he was driving a white sports car. We didn't get no make or model but it was one of the big expensive jobs, foreign make."

Turk asked Lavallo, "Did you see his car?"

"No."

"Was he wearing an overcoat when you saw him?"

The underboss shook his head decisively. "No. I didn't get much of a look, we was just bangin' away at each other, but he wasn't in no overcoat. The black part fits, though."

One of the crew chiefs idly asked. "Wonder why the guy's so hung up on black. Does he think he's gonna psycho somebody?"

"He wears black," Turk said grimly, "for the same reason the commandos did. He works mostly at night, and you don't usually see 'im until he wants you to. And you better remember that."

"Goddam clown," Lavallo muttered.

"Pardon me, but he sure is *not* no clown," Turk corrected the *Caporegime*. "And we better all remember that." His eyes snapped to a crew chief. "Okay, Bernie. Maybe we got something here, maybe not. You got to find out what." A blunt forefinger was tracing a path on the map. "The way I'd read it, he come down off of the freeway right here, on his way in from the L & A hit. Mr. Lavallo says it was about five-thirty, the hit. That would give him time to. . . . Sure, it fits. So I want a clean sweep of every hotel and motel in that area. You know what to look for."

"It's snowing pretty bad outside right now," Lavallo commented. "I hear the roads are closing up north and storm warnings are flying all up and down the lake."

"So what are you thinking?" Turk asked him.

"I'm thinking what you said awhile ago was exactly right. I bet the guy has crawled into a hole to ride out the storm. I'm thinking your chances of finding him tonight are about one in a million."

Turk smiled and replied, "I guess you're right, Mr. Lavallo. But we got to ride those odds, eh?"

"Right, *you* got to," Lavallo said. "Me, I'm going home and sleeping out this million-to-one pass."

"You do that, Mr. Lavallo," Turk told him.

The underboss hurried out, waving quietly to familiar faces along the line.

Turk turned a relieved grin to a crew chief. "Okay, get that hotel crew busy. There ain't *no* storm, *no* where, going to keep me off of this Bolan's ass. We're going to nail this guy, Bernie. We're going to nail him *tonight.*"

The storm signals were flying, for everyone but Larry the turkey-maker. He was brewing a personal storm of his own making.

For that matter, so was Pete the Hauler.

5: JUNGLE LESSON

Bolan sat cross-legged on the bed, staring thoughtfully at the still form beside him. He gently nudged a shiny hip and said, "Hey . . . sleepyhead . . . time to rise and shine."

Her eyelids fluttered half open and she peered out at him through curling lashes. "Not asleep," she murmured. "Are you an angel?"

"Not hardly," he replied, grinning. "Do I look like one?"

She smiled back and gently stirred herself. "Not hardly. But if this is heaven, then you must be an angel."

He said, "Wrong on both counts. This is hell, lady. Or it's likely to be if we don't get moving."

Her eyes opened fully. "But I thought . . ."

"That we were home clean?" He shook his head. "This is just a rest area. We've got to be up and on. And the sooner the better." He rolled off the bed and went into the bath, returning immediately with his clothing.

"Gosh, you're a beautiful thing," she told him. "I think men should be required to run around like that all the time. It would sure brighten us girls' lives."

Bolan grinned and said, "That's carrying women's lib a bit far, isn't it?" He reversed his thermal skinsuit, turning the white inner surface to the outside, and began getting into it. "You'd better get it in gear. I'm leaving here in five minutes, with or without you."

"Five *minutes*!" she squealed. She leapt off the bed and dashed into the bath, calling back, "I thought you told me you had some sort of deal. About me, I mean."

He replied, "For what it's worth, yeah."

"Well just what *is* it worth?"

"It's a confusion factor, that's about all. I figure it may have bought us a couple of hours, and maybe a temporarily divided enemy camp. But we can't bet on even that."

"But surely we're safe *here*!" she cried. "I mean, after all, they can't search every room in Chicago, can they. *Can* they?"

Bolan strapped on the Beretta and told her, "Sure they can. That's the whole game, at this point. I threw down the gauntlet, and it hit them right across the face. At the time, I hadn't planned . . ." He paused and changed the direction of his explanation. "I changed the battle plan a little—and now it's their offensive, not mine. And, yeah, they'll be searching."

"Well, what are we going to do?" She emerged from the bath and went to the parcels Bolan had brought in earlier. Her eyes collided with the Beretta and skipped hastily away.

He slipped into his shirt and muttered, "Does the gun bother you?"

"That's the first real gun I've ever seen," she said. "I had no idea they looked so . . . so menacing."

"The word is *deadly*," he told her. "And this one's a jewel. I picked it up in France. Worked in the trigger for a four-pound pull, which means she blasts if you breathe hard on her. She'll target eight rounds into a two- inch grouping from thirty yards, and it takes less than a

60

second to reload. Carries nine-millimeter Parabellum hi-shockers, and she'll put a crease in a guy that would make a tommy-gun green with envy."

"Why are you telling me all this?" she asked quietly.

"Just want you to know what you're traveling with. If I suddenly yell *down*, that means you de-materialize and reassemble yourself on the ground or on the floor, wherever you happen to be. It means that the Beretta Belle is leaving her leather behind, and she comes out blasting, and we don't want any beloved flesh getting into her path. Understood?"

Jimi murmured, "Understood," and withdrew a scruff of silk from a paper bag. "Oh wow," she said. "Heart shaped panties. Where'd you say you bought these things?"

He said, "Don't change the subject. I want you to—"

"I liked that part about beloved flesh," she told him impiously. "And don't worry about me getting in your way. If you yell *down*, I'll just faint. Would that put me out of the way quick enough?"

Bolan said, "Not hardly. I could be working on the second load before you could topple over. When I say *down*, I mean *this*!" He showed her what he meant, going from full perpendicular to flat horizontal in a heartbeat.

The girl's eyelids fluttered. She sank to her knees and showed him a teasing smile. "Now I know where you got your boudoir prowess," she said. "You learned it on the battlefield."

He got to his feet and barked, "Do it!"

Her eyes fluttered some more and she replied, "You're really serious."

"I've never been more serious in my life. It's a jungle out there we have to get through, Jimi. You have to

61

know how to survive it." He pulled her upright and said, "Okay, now show me. *Down!*"

Jungle Jimi went *down,* then she rolled onto her back and lay there laughing. "I can't wait to show the Foxy Ladies," she giggled. "How'd I do?"

"Okay," he growled. Again he pulled her upright, turned his back on her, said "Get dressed, dammit," and took two steps across the room. Then he cried, *"Down!"* and flung himself to the floor in a lightning scramble, rolling back towards the girl with the Beretta out at full extension.

She was standing where he'd left her, frozen, the heart-shaped panties in her hands, gaping at him.

"Dammit, I just cut your legs off at the knees," he told her.

"I—I wasn't expecting you to say it," she explained.

"That's the whole point." He got up and found his trousers and put them on. "That's the way it happens, when it happens." He snapped his fingers. "Like that. And you better be flexed to react like that, if you mean to stay alive."

The seriousness of the situation was beginning to impress itself on her. She carried the clothing to the bed and began dressing. Her hands trembled, and she was having other difficulties. Bolan went over to help her. "What a rotten end to such a lovely honeymoon," she said miserably.

"It beats dying," he pointed out.

Tears sprang to her eyes. "Oh Mack, how can you live this way?" she wailed.

He dug out a bra and hung it on her. "If I don't live this way," he softly explained, "I die quick."

"But on and on and on. Isn't there any end to it?"

He fastened the bra and told her, "Sure, there's an

end. But I'm in no hurry to get there."

"It's like the law of the jungle," she whispered. "Survival of the fittest, kill or be killed, no quarter, damn the torpedoes, all that."

"That," he whispered back, "is exactly what I've been trying to tell you. Now listen to me. The storm has hit. All the airlines are grounded. The highways are closing. Trains have stopped running. There's no way I can get you out of this town. And we can't hole up, that gives the mob all the advantage of the hunt. We have to go out there, and we have to keep moving, and we have to keep alive. Out there, Jimi, in that jungle. Are you fit to survive?"

Bolan had achieved the desired effect. The soft shoulders stiffened and fiercely she said, "You're damn right."

"Then stop shaking and start dressing. Every minute could be vital."

"I'm in your way, aren't I," she declared quietly. "I'm really just jeopardizing you."

"No," he lied. "You're giving me a better reason to stay alive." And maybe it wasn't all lie.

She pulled a pants-suit from the boutique box and held it to her. "It's lovely," she said. "Everything you do is lovely, isn't it."

He grinned and told her, "Sure, I even kill lovely."

"But only in the jungle," she said, trying to sound cheerful again.

"That's right."

She lunged forward suddenly and planted a wet kiss on his lips. "Caught you, you're dead," she whispered.

"Huh uh," he replied. "Alive. *Totally* alive."

She pushed him away and watched him from beneath lowered lashes as she stepped into the clothing. "Girls have jungles too, you know," she said. "Just wait 'till I get *you* into *mine*."

"Hell, I've been there," he said, grinning.

"Well, just wait 'till I get you *back* in there."

Bolan turned quickly away to conceal the emotion surging into his eyes, covering with a noisy inspection of the Beretta. He hoped with everything he had that he would walk Jimi's beautiful jungle again one day. Right now, though, he had to safely escort her through his own.

And that, he knew, was going to take some doing.

6: AND INTO THE NIGHT

Larry Turk leaned forward to pat his wheelman's shoulder and to instruct him, "Pull up over here, Gene."

The driver nodded and eased the big car to the curb, halting diagonally across from the entrance to the Town Acres Motor Lodge. Visibility in the swirling, wind-driven snowfall was practically zero, and even the glittering neon tower of Town Acres was no more than a phosphorescent-like glow hovering in the sky.

Another vehicle nosed in behind Turk's car. Seconds later, crew chief Bernie Tosca blew into the rear seat beside Larry Turk, bringing in a puff of snowflakes with him.

Turk brushed delicately at his pants leg and growled, "What a night to be out, eh?"

"Yeah." Tosca wiped the freezing moisture from his face and blew into his hands. "That's the place over there, huh?"

"That's it. Homer Peoples has the girl concession here. You know Homer?"

Tosca smiled nastily and replied, "Who doesn't. Is this a sure make, boss?"

"Not all that sure," Turk told him. "Homer saw this white Ferrari in the parking lot. He went to the desk to check it out. Car has Indiana plates, and the desk had 'em registered as Mr. and Mrs. William Franklin, from Indianapolis. Homer couldn't get no more. The day shift had gone home and nobody on duty remembered seeing the guy."

"Homer played it quiet, I hope," Tosca said.

"He said he did. The room number is B-240. That'll be south end, upstairs."

"We have to go in through the lobby? I don't remember this layout."

"Naw, there's four ways up from outside—two stairs going up from the parking lot, that's on this side, and two going up from the—whatta ya call it, the courtyard?—anyway, there's four outside stairs."

"Oh yeah, I think I remember now. All these rooms open on the outside, upstairs they got this iron porch that circles around the joint. I got it now."

"Okay," Turk said, "but listen. I want some boys in the lobby, and I want boys on all four stairways. I want no fuck-ups, Bernie."

"Don't worry, there won't be any."

"You take him *inside*. I mean that. He gets out in this mess and we might never see him again."

"What if he ain't there?"

"Then you sit and wait, and send somebody down to tell me. And also you send me whoever else *is* in there."

"Right." Tosca nervously lit a cigarette and leaned against the door. "You want this Bolan alive?"

"If you catch him in bed with his pants down, sure. But don't take no chances. If he's ready for a fight, just bring me his head and his hands, that's all I need. And don't leave *no*body else alive. You know?"

"Right. Here's what I'm going to do, Turk. I'm sending two cars in right here, into the parking lot, as insurance. And I'm taking Bobby Teal and Joe the Bouncer with me up the south stairs. The rest of the boys I'll have covering the other ways out."

Turk growled, "You better leave a couple of plug men at the bottom of *your* stairs, too."

"Okay, yeah, I'll do that."

"Okay, great," Turk said. "And just in case it *all* falls to hell, I'll be waiting right here. Me and Willie Thompson."

A man seated in the front beside the driver snickered and raised the snout of a Thompson submachine gun into view. "I hope it all falls to hell," he commented.

"Fuck you, Willie," Bernie Tosca said, and flung himself back into the snowstorm.

Larry Turk chuckled and again touched the wheelman's shoulder. "Okay, let's ease down in front of that exit."

The heavy vehicle crunched slowly along the snowpacked street, taking station for a rub-out. "You smelling blood, Willie?" Turk asked, still chuckling.

"Hell, boss, I can almost taste it," Wille Thompson replied.

The ghostly glow of headlamps loomed suddenly in front of them as a large car, moving cautiously in the restricted visibility, swung past and into the motel entrance. For one electric instant the occupants were visible in the lights of Larry Turk's vehicle. The field general's chuckles stifled into a grunted, "Christ! Wasn't that . . . ?"

"It sure as hell was!" the wheelman confirmed.

"Who?" said Willie Thompson. "I didn't see 'em. Who was it?"

Larry Turk was swearing loudly to nobody in particular.

67

The wheelman told Wille Thompson, "That was Pete the Hauler. With a car-full of boys."

Some of the parcels which Bolan had brought into the motel room had been for himself. The black suit and overcoat had given way to a white, heavy-weather jumpsuit, water-resistant and tightly cuffed at ankles and wrists. Over this he wore a light but warm hooded jacket, also white, and gray rubberized boots with thermal linings.

His concern at the moment was for Jimi James. He gave her a final critical inspection and declared, "I guess you'll do."

"I guess I'd do for an Artic expedition," she replied drily. Bolan had stuffed her into several layers of clothing—frilly underthings next to the skin followed by a thermal suit similar to Bolan's own, then the heavy wool pants-suit and knee-high boots, all in white. A hiplength ski jacket, muffler, cap and gloves completed the outfit—and she was feeling a bit put out by the entire thing. "From the sublime to the ridiculous," she groused. "Where are our snowshoes?"

Bolan ignored the wisecrack and tested his access to the Beretta. Jimi could see the displeasure in his eyes. She said, "Don't mind me. When I get scared I get sarcastic."

"I don't mind you," he assured her. "It's this outfit . . . it's a bit clumsy." He grinned and added, "Look who's demanding perfection," then he hit the light switch and the room went dark.

In a quavery voice, Jimi asked, "Did you say *down?*"

He chuckled. "No, I didn't."

"Why are we standing here in the dark?"

"Can you see me?" he asked her.

"No."

"When you can, we'll go out."

"Oh," she said, small voiced. Then—"Are you always this careful?"

"I try to be."

A moment later she advised him, "I guess my eyes are adjusted. I can see you. Sort of."

He said, "Fine," and cracked the door open.

"M-Mack?"

"Yeah?"

"If I die . . . if we die . . ."

"Think *living*, Jimi—not dying." He made a quick doorway recon, then took her by the hand and pulled her outside with him.

The choking snow enveloped them immediately and they moved swiftly along the upper porch to the stairway. Again Bolan paused to get the lie and the feel of the environment.

Jimi gasped, "What's the—?"

"Hush," he whispered.

The engine of an automobile could be heard idling somewhere just below. The motel's outside lights were no more than faint and isolated specks of useless luminescence. Bolan's hand went to the railing of the steel stairway, fingertips lightly pressed to the dry underside.

They stood that way for perhaps thirty seconds, then Bolan quickly propelled her along the porch and pressed her against the side of the building. "Not a sound," he whispered. "Not even a harsh breath."

Jimi knew that the Beretta was in his hand and that he was waiting for something of which she had not yet become aware. She covered her mouth with a gloved hand and huddled to the wall, blinking away the snowflakes which were trying to invade her eyes. Then she became aware that Bolan had moved slightly away from her. She reached out to touch him—he gave the questing hand a reassuring squeeze, and then he was gone.

Seconds later she heard voices, muted and ghostly in the wind, without source of direction, but apparently drawing steadily nearer.

"Jesuschrist I can't see a goddam thing."

"Quiet, just be quiet."

"What if we get lost?"

"Whoever heard of getting lost on a fuckin' stairway?"

"I heard of a guy getting lost in his own backyard in a blizzard once. They found him the next morning, froze to death, ten feet from his own back door."

"Dammit, you guys heard me say be quiet!"

Three voices, evidently ascending the stairway. Jimi was learning to understand the signs of the jungle.

"Did that pimp say B-240?"

"Don't call 'im no pimp. He's a pers'nal friend of th' boss, you better not let him hear—"

"Pimp, shrimp—the next guy to say a word is gettin' a bullet right inna ear! Now dammit, shut up!"

There was little doubt as to the meaning of that muffled conversation, even for a jungle novice such as Jimi James. And suddenly her mind seemed to become as one with Mack Bolan's. She knew that he was poised there, near the top of that stairway, his eyes straining against the blinding snow, all of his senses finely tuned into that split-second of opportunity to pounce like the great jungle cat that he was. And, in that startling instant, Jimi understood the inner man that was Mack

70

Bolan as perhaps no other person had. Her fear, in that moment of understanding, gave way to an inner calm awaiting the inevitable.

And the inevitable came quickly, as Bolan had promised. A shivering voice, very close now, muttered, "Let's see, B-240. I wonder which way that would be."

A returning voice of cold steel suggested, "To your left."

"*Huh?*"

"*Wh—?*"

Jimi might have missed the quiet phuttings of the Beretta against the background of storm noises if she had not also seen the lances of flame that came so closely together as to almost be connected—and, yes, she knew now about suddenness.

An almost unbearably drawn-out quiet descended. A sign above Jimi's head creaked with the wind—now and then the murmuring idle of the automobile engine was brought in on the wind. She fought down an impulse to call out Bolan's name, and instead conjured a picture of him standing at the head of that stairway, taking its pulse at the railing, his animal senses flaring out into the storm to draw in impressions which perhaps would not come to an ordinary person.

And suddenly his hand was on her's and his lips, close to her ear, were instructing her, "Let's go, quietly."

She went, and quietly, one hand in Bolan's, his body partially shielding her's. He led her around the cluster of fallen soldiers and they began the descent.

Bolan stiffened suddenly, about halfway down, and Jimi reflexively made herself small behind him. Then she became aware of the sounds that had halted him—another murmur of voices, somewhere out in the storm, rising frequently to angry tones—an occasional glimpse of auto headlamps shimmering through the vertical blanket of snowflakes. She could not be certain if she was seeing multiple sets of lights or if a single pair were creating optical illusions.

Then Bolan was tugging at her and they went on, cautiously planting their feet and pausing at each step before progressing to the next one. And the voices were becoming clearer.

A heavy one, sounding angry and vexed, was declaring, ". . . tells me where I go and where I don't go. You go back and tell 'im that."

Another, respectful, almost pleading: "It's just that this's no place for an important man like you t'be, Mr. Lavallo. Turk just don't want you exposing yourself needlessly."

"I know what Turk don't want, Bernie, and you better remind 'im who he's dickin' around with. And you better remind yourself."

Bolan and Jimi were off the stairway now and moving past the headlamps and voices—close, so close. The snow was drifting into kneehigh ridges along the line of parked vehicles, and they were following one of these ridges. Bolan was moving surely and swiftly now, and again Jimi marvelled at his finely developed instincts or whatever it was propelling him into the blind chaos of the night.

A formless dark shape materialized in their path; Jimi recoiled at about the same instant that the Beretta coughed and another pencil-flame lanced the storm. The blob gave off a "Whuf" and dematerialized—and on they went. Jimi stumbled over something soft lying across her path. She caught her breath and her balance at the same time, shivering in the knowledge that she had stepped on an arm or a leg of a man who, seconds earlier, had been alive and sentient.

The voices of the night had suddenly shut themselves off, then the angry one could be heard nervously inquiring, "Did you hear that? Didn't you hear something?"

"Sounds will fool you in this kind of weather, Mr. Lavallo. Really now, why don't you——?"

"Naw, that's a sound you never forget. It's that blaster with a special kind of silencer, I think. That bastard's out here somewhere, I bet. I'm gonna call in my boys."

"God, Mr. Lavallo, don't——"

That voice was lost in the sudden loud blasting of an automobile horn. Another blob of motion appeared off to Jimi's right, crunching snow and breathing hard in a hurried transit. She understood then Bolan's selection of white clothing for this night; they were probably invisible, she was thinking. These other people were no more than shapeless patches of a darker mass against the inpenetratable white background.

A loud voice nearby was demanding, "Shut it off! Shut off that goddam horn if you have to shoot 'im!"

And then Jimi understood that the enemy were all around them—this was like a game of blind man's buff, with everybody as the blind men and Mack Bolan operating with some sort of a personal inner radar. The night had come alive with running feet on crunching snow, startled exclamations, muffled shouts, and the building sounds of a growing confusion.

Bolan had come to an abrupt halt, and somehow Jimi knew that he had located the Ferrari. She swung about to get behind him, and found herself sprawling forward suddenly, off-balance and falling over a large object which she immediately recognized as the front end of an automobile.

Bolan's strong grip was jerking her upright and stabilizing her, and a worried voice closeby was inquiring, "Hank? What's the matter?"

"Nothin', I thought it was you," came the slightly distant reply from the rear of the car.

Then Bolan's lips were at Jimi's ear and a harsh *"down"* was echoing inside her skull. Without quite realizing how she had arrived there, Jimi found herself lying in the snow and rolling madly for the protection of the vehicle.

The Beretta Belle was coughing a soft symphony of destruction amidst the louder crashes of several pistols. Something hit the snow beside her outflung hand and she instinctively seized it and recognized in the feel of it an expended ammunition clip from the Beretta.

She remembered Bolan's cool words, ". . . and it takes less then a second to reload," and she understood what was transpiring and felt better for the knowledge.

Phuttings and booms and muffled cries and grunts, shouts in the night, revving auto engines, madness—and then something hard was being pressed into her gloved hand and Bolan's reassuring tones were ordering her into the Ferrari.

Jimi found herself responding subconsciously, unlocking the car and sliding in behind the wheel, praying for heavenly direction in the technique of starting this strange vehicle—then the powerful engine was somehow roaring in a half-throttle idle and she was flinging herself into the adjacent seat as Bolan leapt in beside her and they lurched across the snowdrift.

He commanded, "On the floor, Foxy"—and she was

already there and the Ferrari was spinning forward into the suffocating night, without lights, perhaps without hope, but with absolute blazing determination at the wheel.

Angrily sizzling things were penetrating the car, striking with jarring thumps and tearing through its metallic skin, shattering its glass, shredding its upholstery. Jimi cringed against the floorboards and listened to the Beretta, now unsilenced, blasting defiantly into the entrapment. She heard her man grunt with some unidentified pain and, an instant later, his warning shout: "Get braced, hang on!"

And then he was lying across the seat just behind her, one arm looped powerfully about her curled body. In a flash of understanding, she knew that they were about to crash into something, and the last sound Jimi heard before the rending impact was the growling chatter of a machine gun and a new onslaught of furious projectiles punching into the Ferrari.

"*On and on and on,*" she had complained earlier. "*Isn't there any end to it?*"

And he had replied, "*Sure, there's an end—but I'm in no hurry to get there.*"

They had, it seemed, gotten there, and together, and it was probably all her fault. Even through the red fog that was enveloping her, though, Jimi knew that she was definitely *en rapport* with the inner man that was Mack Bolan. There were no regrets in that bond, no condemnation. And if she had to die this night, then at least she would die knowing love. No, there were no regrets.

Bolan had not been operating entirely on instinct. With a foresight engendered by a constant battle for

75

survival, he had routinely staked out his retreat route from that motel room, posting in his mind the various details and mentally rehearsing a withdrawal under combat conditions. The trip from the door of his room to the parked Ferrari had become translated into so many steps north, so many west, so many north again—and he had an equivalent picture of the route out of that parking lot, but oriented to elapsed time in a moving vehicle. Long before the storm descended, he had burned into his mind every detail of his physical surroundings.

Superimposed upon this mental map was Bolan's intimate familiarity with the enemy and their standard operating procedures. The final result—his success in breaking out of the trap—could be regarded as a sort of "battlefield intuition," built of conditioned instincts and a subliminal response to a rehearsed situation. This is the goal of all military training—in such a typical crisis situation, in which the individual's life or the success of a mission is hanging in the balance, the thinking mind moves aside for the crisis-response of trained reflexes—and this is what carried Bolan and the Ferrari and its passenger to that grinding moment at the exit from the motel parking lot.

Thus, what appeared to Jimi James to be phenomenal perceptions in a blinding storm was actually a high exercise of military preparedness and training. One deviation from his prescribed path would have rendered Bolan as blind and ineffective as the other parties to that chaos; it was *foresight,* not ESP, that guided this warrior unerringly to his vehicle. And it was this same quality of the military mind, but now translated into an acute sense of timing and the burnt-in memory of a traffic pattern, that guided his vehicle out of its resting place and along the route of retreat.

This method did not, of course, account for incidental misplaced vehicles blocking the path, banks of drifted snow, a war party of enemy infantry firing wildly into the night, and various other nuisances that could crop up. The Ferrari, as it came charging blindly out of its nest, sent a pair of gun-toting pedestrians hurtling off into diverging flights, sideswiped a larger vehicle which had been idling in the traffic lane, punched down a metal post marking the turn toward the exit, and struck head-on another soldier who had been running blindly into the sounds of battle. And all along this course, the vehicle was taking repeated hits from a determined handgun fusillade; Bolan was required to pilot the car, attempt an effective return-fire, and maintain cognizance of his time-track—all with the same mind and at the same time.

Incredible as this may seem, Bolan might have succeeded in making a clean breakaway had it not been for the final enemy factor—the foresight of another trained warrior, Larry Turk, and the "plug car" just outside the motel exit.

Turk had left this "safety plug" in the capable hands of Willie Thompson, while he descended wrathfully upon the early sounds of confusion emanating from the parking area. It had been his angry voice demanding the cessation of horn signals from Lavallo's vehicle; Bernie Tosca had not yet had time to get his crew positioned into the trap stations, and Turk was reading Lavallo's interference as the highest form of treason.

Meanwhile, Willie Thompson had exercised a prerogative of his own and ordered the plug vehicle onto station directly blocking the exit from the motel. Both he and the wheelman had then taken cover behind the street side of the car and awaited developments.

It seems likely that *any* vehicle attempting to leave the motel area would have been accorded the same reception which Bolan received. Willie was targeting entirely on audibles, and when the Thompson opened fire, it was purely a reflexive attack upon a moving vehicle which no one could actually see.

Bolan could, however, see the blazing eruptions from the chopper's muzzle and the shadowy bulk of vehicle from behind which they were emerging, and his reflexes sent him accelerating into the blockade as the only possible hope for neutralizing this latest challenge. He was lying across the front seat with one arm protectively clasping his floored passenger when the Ferrari sheared into the heavier Mafia car, and he had the passenger-door open and was snaking to the ground even while the sports car was quivering into the rebound.

The chopper had fallen silent and someone nearby was groaning with pain. Bolan was collecting himself, silently calling roll on his various parts and finding them all present and functioning, though his ears were ringing and there was a numbness in the area of his left shoulder. He carefully extricated Jimi from the wreckage and slung the unconscious girl onto his good shoulder.

The sounds of chaos were drifting over from the parking lot and an anxious voice very closeby called, "Willie? Are you okay?"

"I think my arms are broke," came a groaning response. "Don't worry about me, check out that Bolan. Make sure he's dead."

"You got 'im, I know you got 'im."

"Bullshit, you check 'im out. Don't take nothin' for granted."

78

The hood over the Ferrari's engine compartment was crumpled and askew. Bolan slipped the Beretta's muzzle into the opening and squeezed off three quick rounds in a searching pattern, then quickly backstepped as flames whooshed out. He collided with a fast-moving figure who was hurrying around the tail of the Mafia vehicle as the groaning man cried, "Gene! Get me outta here, we're on fire!"

But Gene had problems of his own, in the form of a hot muzzle at his throat and a coldly insistent voice in his ear, demanding, "Let's find some wheels, Gene."

In a choked voice, Turk's wheelman suggested, "There oughta be a couple cars right up the street."

"Okay, let's go," Bolan commanded.

As they trudged away, a snarling voice from somewhere inside the din of the motel parking lot was shouting, "Goddammit, hold your fire, what the hell you think you're shooting at? Bernie, where the hell are you?"

"Over here, Turk—I think the bastard got past us."

"Are you crazy? Can't you hear anything? He's out there dueling with Willie! Get your boys out there!"

"Christ, boss, I can't even see where I'm at."

"*Fuck* where you're at! You get it out there where *he's* at!"

Where Bolan was "at," however, was now beyond the immediate reach of the headhunting crew. An expert wheelman was transporting him and his unconscious companion in an appropriated crew wagon, away from the combat zone, deeper into the jungle of survival, onward into the night.

Bolan was working on his girl, and presently she roused, and found herself in Bolan's arms, and she murmured, "Are you an angel?"

He smiled, remembering, and replied, "Not hardly. You got a bump on the head. Feeling okay?"

She gave him a glowing-eyes nod. "On and on and on," she whispered. "I love you, Mack. I hope we *never* find the end."

Bolan pointedly ignored the declaration of love. He ran a finger through a bullet hole in her ski jacket and gruffly told her, "You came that close to the end, Foxy. About a sixteenth of an inch, I'd say."

Too close, much too close, and Bolan realized that the war had hardly begun. He could not expose this girl to any more of it. He would have to find a place to stow her, and then he would have to get this war into gear and—one way or another—get it finished.

"You're hurt," she had just discovered. "Your neck, it's—"

"Just a nick," he assured her. Bolan was not concerned about the scratch at his neck. It was the old wound in the shoulder that was giving him fits—his souvenir of New York. With two hands his task was going to be difficult enough—with *one* hand . . .

The wheelman was throwing him uneasy glances via the rearview mirror. Bolan sighed and said, "Okay, Gene, end of trip for you. Stop at the next sign of life. And don't look so worried, I'm going to turn you loose. With a message. You deliver it straight, and you deliver it completely, or I'll come looking for you."

"Sure, Mr. Bolan," the wheelman replied. "You got my word, I'll take a message anywheres you want."

"You'll take it to the *Capo's,* Gene. All of them. And to the Chicago Four. You tell them that Bolan is busting their sanctum city wide open tonight. Tonight, understand?"

"Yessir, I got that."

"And I'm taking them, too. All of them, all the bosses. Their free ride ends tonight."

"I'll tell 'em that, Mr. Bolan."

"I know who they are and I know where they are. And not one of them will see another sunrise. Are you reading me, Gene?"

"Yessir. You're wiping 'em all out tonight."

"That's it. This storm is my friend, their enemy. You make sure that message gets delivered. All of it."

"I'll sure make sure, Mr. Bolan. You got my word."

"Okay. What's this up ahead?"

"I believe we're coming up on the Merchandise Mart, sir."

"Fine. You leave us there. You stop the car, you get out, you disappear damn quick, and you don't look back once. Reading me?"

"Yessir, I been reading you right along."

Yes, Gene the wheelman had been reading him. Great. So he'd set himself an impossible goal, he'd challenged himself to produce something unproduceable. But that was what this rotten war was made of, and Bolan had to get it into gear . . . and finished. One way or another, the War for Chicago would end tonight.

He gently squeezed the girl's hand and told her, "No end for you, Jimi. Not here, not in this lousy war."

"I end where you end," she murmured.

Bolan hoped not. With everything in him, he fervently hoped not.

7: THE COURSE

The sign outside the modest North Side residence had announced the offices of Joseph Berger, "tax consultant." According to a brief note in Bolan's intelligence book, however, Joseph Berger was actually Leopold Stein, a brilliant Chicago attorney who, in his own way, had also waged a war against the mob . . . and lost.

Bolan was familiar with most of the details of Stein's story. He'd been a successful and respected lawyer, well-established in a comfortable practice, when he launched his "citizen's campaign" and began crusading for "a free Chicago." For two years he had weathered threats, beatings, economic pressures, and various forms of political harassment while he dug into and exposed the various links in the chains that held his city bound. And when he began to step on overly sensitive toes, the cancer of power focussed its attention on this insignificant upstart long enough to finally crush the source of irritation. Or so it must have thought. Stein had been indicated on charges of fraud and criminal conspiracy, disbarred from practicing law, financially ruined, physically maimed, crippled, and finally reduced to the shame of hiding under an assumed name.

Now forty-seven years of age, the plucky crusader looked sixty. His hair was snow-white. Prolonged pain and mental anguish had ravaged the once strong face—now heavily-scarred and bearing a leather patch over an empty eyesocket. He was partially paralyzed and confined to a wheelchair—but Leo Stein was still alive and, in his own way, fighting back. He spent most of his time now preparing legal briefs and background files, anonymously, and forwarding them to various grand juries and crime commissions in Illinois and neighboring states. According to Bolan's notes, Stein was the foremost living authority on mob operations in and around Chicago—it was said that he understood the interconnections of criminal influence even better than most men inside the mob.

In Bolan's thinking, this man had given more than anyone could reasonably ask. And so it was with an air of apology that the Executioner told him, "We need your help, Mr. Stein."

"Oh, I doubt that," the attorney replied, inspecting his visitor with a critical gaze from the one good eye. "I've been following your war with interest, Mr. Bolan. I don't entirely approve, but . . . well, I have to admit that your approach seems more effective than mine." His attention returned to Jimi James, and he added, "And certainly you're far more admirably supported than I."

The girl's eyes dropped. She murmured, "I'm afraid I'm just so much excess baggage."

"What do you want?" Stein asked Bolan, suddenly all business.

"Someone is helping you remain covered," Bolan replied, just as directly. "I want you to ask them to do the same for Miss James."

"I'll do that," Stein replied without hesitation. "What else?"

"I want protection for her right away, tonight."

"You mean that you want her off your hands."

"Think of it any way you like. I just want the girl protected."

"You don't feel capable of doing that yourself?"

The guy was probing him, and Bolan knew it. He said, "No sir. The chase is getting pretty hot." He drew an imaginary circle about the bullet hole in Jimi's jacket. "*Too* hot."

"And you have confidence in my security. That's it?"

Bolan nodded. "Yes sir, I have."

"But I'm not all that secure, am I?" the lawyer said quickly.

"Sir?"

"How the hell did *you* find me?"

"Any security can be breached," Bolan replied. "She'd still be a thousand times better off than with me."

"You didn't answer my question," Stein said fiercely.

"No sir, and I don't intend to."

The attorney laughed and turned back to the girl. "All right. Leave her here. I'll see that she's provided for."

Bolan got to his feet. Jimi rose also and quietly told him, "I think I'd rather not."

"There isn't that much choice," Bolan quietly replied.

Her eyes fell and she said, "I—I guess you're right. You don't need me on your coattails."

A muscle rippled in Bolan's jaw. He steeled himself and replied, "That's right. Not tonight, that's for sure."

"H-how will we ever find each other again?" she asked in a barely audible voice.

"I'll find you," Bolan promised.

Stein coughed and drily observed, "He found *me*." He threw back his head and yelled, *"Missy!"*

A cute kid of about sixteen appeared immediately in the doorway to the office. Stein told his visitors, "This is my daughter. She answers to *Missy*. Missy, say hello to the pretty lady and get her out of here for awhile. I have some business to discuss with the troubled gentleman."

Bolan showed Jimi a reassuring smile and nodded his head. "Go ahead," he murmured. "We'll say goodbye later."

Jimi accompanied the youngster into the living quarters, pausing just inside the doorway to throw Bolan a wistful glance. He again nodded his head, and she went on.

Stein had moved his wheelchair to a low buffet and was busying himself with a silver service. "Come and get it," he called over. "I can't play the perfect host in this rig."

Bolan went over and accepted a steaming mug of coffee. "Thanks," he said, "it's just what I need."

"You need more than that, but it'll have to do for now. Go on and sit down. I'll be with you in a second."

Bolan took the coffee to an easy chair and carefully sipped it, finding that it was liberally laced with something more stimulating than mere caffeine. The attorney rolled over to the desk and told his guest, "That'll brighten your perspectives a bit, though. Tell me, Mr. Bo—aw to hell with that, let's get directly to first names. Tell me, Mack, what do you think your chances are of busting this town?"

Bolan again sipped the coffee before replying, then: "From one combatman to another, Leo, I guess it's about a chance in a million."

Stein soberly nodded his head. "About the way I

count it. So why'd you come? Why Chicago, of all places?"

Bolan offered his host a cigarette, got declined, lit one for himself. He sighed and said, "After New York, I guess Chicago was a must. I ran into something there that really shook me up. You ever hear of a *Cosa di tutti Cosi*?"

"That translates, roughly, as . . ."

"The Big Thing, or Thing of All Things," Bolan helped.

Stein shook his head. "Sounds very romantic, but no—I've never heard of anything like that around here."

"Picture," Bolan said quietly, "this entire nation chained the way Chicago is."

Stein was evidently picturing it. Presently he said, "Well, it's almost that bad already."

"You really think that?"

The lawyer nodded his head. "Sure. They're everywhere, into everything. The legislatures, the congress . . . ward, precincts, cities, counties—from one end of this country to the other. Sure, it's that bad."

"Think about it for a minute, though," Bolan urged. "Think of national party organizations, the federal executive, the senate, the house, justice department . . . all of it. Think of all that completely and *in fact* dominated by the mob. Are we there already?"

"Oh, I'd hardly think that. No, hell no, thank God, things haven't become *that* bad. On the other hand, they're not . . ."

"Not what?" Bolan prompted.

Stein's face was working at an old frustration. "Do you realize the amount of public propaganda that's being issued merely to convince the people of this nation that the syndicate—the Mafia—*does not exist*? It's the most fantastically flagrant public conspiracy I've ever encountered—why hell, it's a Madison Avenue campaign. Despite all the evidence, all the facts, all the sworn testimony, all the official revelations—despite everything that's been done for the past three decades to expose this menace—there are public officials in practically every echelon of government who are swearing and be-damning that the *Cosa Nostra* is purely a creation of the American press."

"They can say it until they're blue in the face," Bolan declared quietly. "That doesn't change anything. I'm not fighting ghosts, Leo."

"Hell, I know that. And anybody with a grain of sense or a spark of honesty knows it, too. I was just drawing a contrast between the Gloomy Gussies and the Pollyannas. You're telling me that the mob is about ready to pull a national coup—these other idiots are trying to—"

"I'm not Gloomy Gussing you about the *tutti Cosi*, Bolan assured his host. "I lucked onto the summit affair, the organizational meet, at a joint out on Long Island. And before I busted it, I heard enough to shiver my underwear down. These guys are going for all the marbles. If they have their way, they'll soon be handpicking even our presidential candidates."

Stein seemed to be chewing the information. Presently he sighed and took a pull at his coffee. "Just last week," he said, "I read where this professor from Columbia or some school back East told us to quit worrying, the Mafia was dying in the generation gap."

Bolan smiled. "I saw that."

"Lord deliver us from the academicians," Stein groused. "This educated fool conducts a 'study' of an individual Italian family and then releases his breathtaking finding that there is no central pattern in the web of organized crime gobbling this country. Where the hell does he get off? Against a million pages of hard evidence—against facts, figures, names, dates, places, against the most overwhelming mass of evidence ever developed anywhere—where the hell does he get off interviewing one little Italian family and . . . Tell me something, Mack. You've been inside the syndicate. Have you ever known *one* of them who would even give you his true name? Huh?"

Bolan chuckled. "Most of them can't even remember their true name," he replied.

"Ugh. *Cosa di tutti Cosi,* eh? Okay, I'll buy. It's the logical next step. But how does that bring you from Long Island to Chicago? What's the tie-in?"

"Chicago's the model city," Bolan replied quietly. "It's the unofficial blueprint for the nationwide thing." He sighed. "I just thought I'd like to try my hand at tearing up the damned blueprint."

"So why don't you hit this Big Thing itself?" Stein queried. "Why fool around with blueprints?"

"What the hell is there to hit?" Bolan muttered. "It's like taking on an invisible octopus. You hack away at it and you *think* you're chopping off a tentacle here and there—but you're never sure—and even if you do succeed in chopping one off, the damned octopus just promptly grows another in its place. I can't hit *things,* Leo. I can only hit *people.*"

"Uh-huh, I guess I get your drift. But that's the fatal weakness of your brand of warfare, Mack. The only way to beat the mob is to remove their avenues of operation. You must destroy the *thing,* the vehicle."

Bolan shook his head. "For me that's impossible, and you know it. Armies of crime-committees and federal agents are working that angle—and, hell, they're all hamstrung. You should be the first man to recognize that. For me, the *thing* is *people,* and they can't hamstring me. Their vehicle and their avenues of operation resolve finally into *people*—rotten, corrupt, grafting, grasping *people.*"

"You can't kill every rotten person in the country, Mack. We'd suddenly have a population explosion in reverse."

"I can't believe that," Bolan muttered. "The rottenness is in that one percent at the core of the thing. They distort and manipulate everything around to the point where simple ordinary people have to get with the system or get out. I don't consider a guy rotten simply because he's trying to get along in the world."

The attorney heaved a deep sigh and told his visitor, "Well, maybe you're right. Maybe I've allowed bitterness and self pity to get the best of me. Or maybe it's just the business I've been in all my life. The practice of law, my young friend, will make a cynic of any man. So all right, you're in Chicago and you're gunning for that one percent of rot at our core. For this town, call it five percent—and that's not bitterness talking, it's experience. But even if it were only one percent . . . do you know how many living souls constitute one percent of this city? We have something around three and a half million people in Chicago proper, about eight million in the metropolitan area. Take one percent of eight million . . . how do you propose to handle eighty thousand people?"

Bolan said, "I don't. That's where you come in."

"A-ha. So I *do* come into it."

Bolan grinned. "Sure. You're the man with the knowledge. You've been feeding info to the crime busters for three years or more. What has it actually accomplished? Try feeding me, for just a minute or two. I won't demand evidence, statistics, legal briefs, depositions, testaments, nothing. I simply want names. I want *nine* names, Leo."

The attorney was showing Bolan a twisted smile. He said, "You want me to become an accessory before the fact—an accomplice to mass murder."

"Call it what you like," Bolan told him.

"What you want me to call is nine names."

Bolan nodded. "I want the Chicago Four, the cartel. I want the two syndicate bosses. I want to know City Jim's real name. And I want the two guys who are finking on the federal and state levels."

Stein's eye was revealing his surprise. He murmured, "You know quite a bit already."

"Not enough," Bolan said. "I need the names, Leo. I need to know the *people*."

Stein sighed. "You want me to finger nine men for execution."

"That's what I want. The same nine who fingered you."

The lawyer looked away for a moment, then he opened a drawer of his desk, withdrew a metal box, unlocked it, and produced a small leather notebook. He placed the book on the desk and told Bolan, "I really don't approve of you. You know that. But I have to admire you. And I think you deserve support—from *some* quarter—hell, from *every* quarter. But I just don't . . . well, call me gutless."

Bolan snorted, outraged at the suggestion. "We should have a country full of such gutlessness," he growled.

"Hiding here," Stein muttered, ". . . like a groundhog,

burrowing into the earth for protection. And now that I have a chance to *really* . . ."

Quietly Bolan observed, "You don't look all that groundhogish to me. Personally, since you brought it up, I'd say you're a bit too brazen about the whole cover. You shouldn't be engaging in a public business. Anyone could walk in here on the most routine business and spot you. You need to be—"

The attorney halted Bolan's monologue with a chuckling protest. He threw a photo on the desk and said, "Know this guy?"

Bolan was looking at the image of a youngish man with curly black hair, good strong facial lines which—while not entirely handsome—were ruggedly appealing. Gleaming eyes revealed an inner sensitivity, a humaneness and good humor that partially softened and dimensioned the man. "No," he said. "Who is he?"

"Me," Stein replied quietly. "Two years ago."

Bolan's eyes met the one good one; he smiled tightly and said, "Okay, yeah, I see you in there now."

"The point," the attorney said, "is that not even my own dear departed wife would know me now. Tell me, Mack—is it a blessing or a curse?"

Bolan fingered his own rugged features, altered by quite a different method. "I guess it's a bit of both," he muttered.

"Yes . . . well . . ." Stein lifted the notebook and dropped it back to the desk. "It's a bit of groundhog too, I'm afraid. I'm sorry, but I won't incriminate myself." He again lifted the notebook and this time slapped it noisily against the desk. "Call it gutlessness, or call it, simply, too damn much reverence for the law. I'm just another kind of learned fool, Mack—first cousin to the academician. But . . . law is my bag, and . . ."

Bolan got to his feet. "I respect your principles, Leo. Thanks, uh, for the coffee." His gaze swung to the door. "And thanks for taking the girl off my hands. Put her in good ones, eh?"

"I almost wish someone would steal this damn notebook," Stein said, ignoring Bolan's parting speech. "I don't know why I keep it locked up. I've sent copies to every damn crime committee in the country—several times, in fact. And still it's business as usual for our one-percenters." He sighed. "I guess I'd consider it good riddance if someone just lifted it, took it off my hands." He again slapped the desk with the book and let it lie there. "Stand still a moment, I'll send your young lady out—but don't expect me back. I detest tearful farewells."

The shattered man wheeled past Bolan, paused, turned back to fix his visitor with the one-eyed stare, and said, "Good luck, Mack. God, be careful. Don't end up like this." Then he wheeled about and rolled quickly out of the room.

Bolan picked up the leather notebook and secured it into the pocket of his jumpsuit. *Thanks, Leopold Stein,* he said to himself. *If I end up half the man you are, I'll consider it one hell of a victory.*

And then Jimi was running through the doorway and into his arms. "I don't mind staying now," she said breathlessly. "He scared me at first, but—well, Missy told me all about it. They threw acid on him, and bombed his home—oh, all sorts of terrible things. I believe they killed his wife, too—Missy's mother—but she only hinted at it, and I didn't want to pry. And—oh Mack!—that whitehaired old man is only forty-seven years old!"

Mack Bolan knew better. The guy was—about a

million years old. And Bolan was gaining on him fast.

"You take care, Foxy," he sternly told her, and he kissed her hard and warm, and then he went out to close some more years between himself and Leopold Stein.

8: THE PENETRATION

Bolan had come to Chicago prepared for all-out war. This professional soldier was well aware that an army is more than mere numbers of men—it is a force, and that force is composed of men, weapons, munitions, mobility factors, provisions, intelligence, and a fully dimensioned capability for loosing destruction. And Mack Bolan, it has been noted, was a one-man army.

He had acquired the Ford van—a small Econoline model which he thought of as his warwagon—at the height of the New York action, and he had brought it into Chicago several days earlier. The first few days upon the new scene of combat had been given to the development of Bolan's "force." He had quietly gathered intelligence, acquired weapons and munitions, outfitted the war-wagon to its maximum capability, and planned the initial attack which would formally "open" the war. His planning beyond that point had been limited to a generalized "play it by ear" approach.

The reverberations now rattling his inner ear were setting the pace and the direction of these further actions. The message issued to Gene the Wheelman had not been dictated by a boastful posturing not with any sense of flamboyant melodrama. The message was a deliberate combat tactic, and it was issued to produce a specific effect—an effect which this one-man army was determined to exploit to the limit.

Also Bolan had not been kidding about his friendship with the storm. A tireless strategist, he had been studying weather maps and forecasts since his arrival in the windy city. The selection of this particular day for the launching of the Chicago War was directly related to the unfolding weather picture—and this winter storm was indeed, in Bolan's view, his friend and the mob's enemy.

And now he had ditched the commandeered Mafia vehicle, he was in possession of a precious notebook crammed with deadly intelligence, and he was in his war-wagon and moving unerringly upon the heartland of the enemy. The time to strike was *now*, and The Executioner was in wipe-out mode.

If Chicago was shivering in the grip of an icy winter storm, the night club belt along South State Street seemed blissfully unaware—or flagrantly disrespect-ful—of the condition. The entire district was in full swing, the accumulated mass of garish neon overcoming the blinding effect of the heavy snowfall as it swirled in on this tenderloin of mid-America—and it would seem that this was the chosen Mecca to which large numbers of Chicagoans trekked to forget the bleakness and discomfort of a city under storm. Indeed, it appeared that this belt of frenetic human activity enjoyed some sort of special treatment from the city which it so admirably supported—nowhere else were the snow-plows and street machinery in such abundant evidence and in such perpetual motion. In a city where "clout" is king (political influence, the "fix") it is perhaps then no coincidence that South State Street is one of those districts referred to in the federal crime report which stated: "The criminal element is in complete control of many establishments serving liquor to patrons and all of the cabarets featuring striptease entertainment in the main Chicago nightlife areas."

One such cabaret, *Manny's Posh*, usually featuring "girls, girls, girls" and catering specifically to the million and a half annual conventioneers visiting the city, tonight stood uncharacteristically darkened and seemingly lifeless. A hand-scrawled sign taped to the front entrance read: "Sorry—Special Party Tonight. Thanks, and try us again."

Inside was indeed a "special party." Glumfaced men congregated at crowded tables and talked in monosyllabic grunts; some jockeyed for positions at the long bar up front, behind which harried bartenders swirled liquids and filled half-gallon beer pitchers for consignment to the table areas.

The small stage near the rear was darkened and deserted except for several men in overcoats who sprawled there in attitudes of relaxed boredom. Behind that stage were several closet-size dressing rooms and a narrow hallway leading to a rear "clubroom" where well-heeled patrons could receive special attentions from the "girls, girls, girls" between shows. The back room was often used as a sex-blackmail and shakedown parlor—and actually produced more revenue than the rest of the cabaret's business combined. This vicious little racket reputedly used real on-duty policemen as the central feature of the shakedown game.

Tonight, however, there were no pigeons and no games in the room behind the stage. On this night, crew chiefs lolled about and talked in low voices of old times and bolder bosses and the troubling uncertainties of

97

living through the night with a madman stalking their streets and threatening to rub out everything that held meaning for their lives.

And in the "sound-proofed back office" at the other side of the club, host Manny Roberts (*nee* Robert Montessi) was fidgeting in the presence of Loop-overlord Jake (Joliet Jake) Vecci and two of his closest lieutenants, Mario Meninghetti—a muscle specialist—and Charley (Pops) Spanno, an important cog in the district's clout machine.

Manny's best booze was on the private bar and Manny himself was on his very best behavior. It was not often that Joliet Jake personally visited the humble *Posh*, though it had been a mob hangout since the doors were first opened back in the fifties. Jake, of course, *owned* the joint and the liquor license and everything that went with it. Manny's arrangement could not be regarded as a partnership—he fronted for Jake and ran the place and took twenty per cent of the net receipts plus all he could steal from his trade—but he was purely a hired hand and Manny was not a man to forget his place.

He had offered Jake his own desk to sit at, declined—handmade cigars from Manhattan, declined—and the best whiskey in the joint, also declined. Manny was running out of things to offer the boss, and he was growing more nervous by the minute.

"Is there anything at all I can get you, Jake?" he asked, breaking a prolonged silence.

"Naw, just sit still, Manny. Christ's sake, this isn't a social call."

"I'm not on the carpet or anything, I hope," Manny wheezed.

Mario Meninghetti snickered and drolly observed,

"He's got a guilt conscience, Jake. I bet he's been knocking down on th' receipts."

Manny Roberts was wordlessly aghast at the suggestion.

"Or padding the clout books," Pops Spanno put in, leering. "I was talking to Sergeant Daniels just yesterday. He was wondering how come his envelope keeps getting thinner."

"Aw you guys cut it out," Jake said calmly. "They're ribbing you, Manny, Christ's sake. We're here on business, not carpeting."

"Well, yeah, I figured—I mean, I put out the closed sign soon as I got your message. And the boys have been coming in regularly all night. And I just been wondering—well, I mean I guess I'd just like to know what's up, Jake."

"What you don't know won't hurt you none, Manny," Joliet Jake quietly declared. "You're not in this so just shut up."

Manny promptly shut up.

The four men sat in silence for several minutes. Then a knuckle signal at the door announced the entrance of a tall, balding man. He wore a gray suit and topcoat and carried a matching gray hat which was quite wet and still clustered with melting snowflakes.

Without looking up, Joliet Jake told the newcomer, "I been waiting here nearly half an hour, Cap'n."

The new arrival removed his coat and hung it on a rack, then pulled up a chair and dropped into it with a tired grunt. "I'll take a double on the rocks, Manny," he said.

Manny made no move to honor the request; the boss was not drinking.

"I said I been here a half an hour," Vecci declared,

speaking slowly and distinctly.

"I got here as quick as I could, Jake," the Captain replied easily. "Hell, I pick up a paycheck from the city, too, you know."

"Sure, and you know why," Vecci snapped back. "Just don't forget who sponsored you on that fat job, Hamilton."

"How could I forget?" The made cop was smiling affably. "Anyway I'm here and I'm sorry I'm late. I see you've got an army gathered out there."

"That's right," Vecci replied. "And they're ready to roll. Where's those assignments?"

The cop produced a notebook from his jacket pocket. He sighed and said, "We have to play this cool, Jake. You know that."

"Don't we always?" Vecci accepted the book and passed it to Pops Spanno. "Here's your teams," he told him. "Now remember, two boys only to a car. They don't interfere until something really breaks, and they try to act like what they're supposed to be. No talking back and forth between theirselves about company business. And if their cars go in somewheres to eat or something, they don't mix around with no other people. They stay with their cops, and they talk *only* to their cops."

Vecci's gaze flashed back to Captain Hamilton. "When's the pick up?"

"Starts at eleven. I've got them spaced five minutes apart. I don't want it looking like a police convention out there."

Vecci nodded his head agreeably. "Great. That gives us—"

He was interrupted by a rapping at the door. He nodded to Manny Roberts, who then called out, "Yeah?"

100

A man pushed his head and shoulders into the room and addressed himself directly to Mario Meninghetti. "There's a phone company guy out here. Says we should check this phone in here."

"What the hell for?" Meninghetti responded.

"It's the storm. The bar phone's dead, boss. He says this one probably is too."

Vecci swore quietly to himself as Manny Roberts scooped up the telephone and announced, "Hell, it is, it's dead."

Vecci rasped, "You tell that ding-a-ling to get it fixed and quick." He turned back to the others and said, "No wonder we ain't been getting no word. God dammit. Dead phones and every other damn thing. What a hell of a night this turns out to be."

A moment later the hardman was again in the doorway to report, "He's fixin' it, boss. Says he's gotta climb the pole."

Pops Spanno grimaced and asked Vecci, "How'd you like to be out climbin' a damn pole on a night like this, Jake?"

"Not me," the Loop boss quietly replied. "I had enough of that hardship crap in the old days. Don't worry, I seen plenty of it. And there's lots of worse things then climbing poles."

Vecci cleared his throat with a harsh gargling sound, gazed at the police captain, and said, "Listen, Ham—I'll be here probably all night, or until the big break at least. If something breaks on your end, I want to know it right away."

"You'll be the first to know," Hamilton assured his sponsor.

Vecci then decided that he would like a drink, after all, and Manny Roberts hastened to set 'em up all

101

around. When the boss drank, everybody drank.

The conversation fell into small talk concerning the storm, the problems of "clouting" the reorganized police department and the new wave of morality in various areas of the city and county governments.

After several minutes another report came from out front. "This 'phone guy says he thinks it's fixed now, but he wants to check it out in there."

Manny Roberts lifted the telephone and said, "Yeah, I got a tone now."

"They got a tone now," the doorway reporter told the outside world. Then he jerked his head in a nod and relayed into the room, "He says he should check it out himself if you wanta make sure."

Jake Vecci decided, "Hell yes, tell 'im to come in and make sure."

The small talk went on, guarded now, as the outsider entered the office and crossed toward the desk, leaving a trail of melting snow along the carpeting. A tool kit was strapped to his waist and climbing spikes were affixed to his lower legs. Vecci drew back to avoid contact with the ice-and-snow-caked figure.

"Pole climbing," Spanno said, chuckling. "In a goddam blizzard yet. What a hell of a way to make a living."

The pole climber smiled agreeably at the Mafia lieutenant and accepted the telephone from Manny Robert's hand, tried to place a call, frowned and tried again, then announced, "Good thing I checked. The outage let the gremlins in."

"Did what?" Manny asked.

The guy was already tearing the telephone apart. "Aw it's the flux field," he explained. "You go dead for a little

102

while, sometimes, and the polarities go haywire. I'll have it fixed in a minute."

"What the hell's a flux field?" Spanno wondered, smiling.

"Get your mind outta th' gutter," Meninghetti suggested. "That's technical talk and way over your head, Pops."

"Okay, technical expert, you tell me what a flux field is," Spanno retorted.

Meninghetti shrugged and replied, "Shit, it's just that stuff that comes outta the flux. Isn't that right, pole-climber?"

The man grinned and said, "Yeah, that's about it."

Vecci sighed and told Manny Roberts, "Give the boy a drink. He looks froze."

The "boy" shook his head at Roberts and said, "No thanks, I'd better not."

"I bet he keeps warm enough, Jake," Spanno suggested. "Christ, he's made up for the South Pole."

Indeed, the "boy" seemed quite well outfitted for pole-climbing, south or north. A heavy white jumpsuit covered him from end to end, and a hooded headpiece tightly encircled his face from mouth to brows, with a button-flap to protect the face itself. This latter feature was presently unbuttoned and swingingly loosely, only partially concealing the reddened and storm-lashed flesh.

Spanno added, "Hell, fella, I wouldn't have your job on a night like this for all the—"

"He's getting overtime," the cop put in. "What're you getting, about double time and a half?"

The "repairman" replied, "No such luck. This's my regular shift."

"Hey, leave the boy alone," Jake Vecci commanded. "He'll never get his job done with all this jawing at him."

"It's okay," Mack Bolan told the *Capo*. "I've got it now."

His audience sat in a strained silence and watched him reassemble the instrument, then he made the test call, grinned and winked at Pops Spanno while he mumbled something into the mouthpiece. He hung up, the phone promptly rang, and he picked it up and mumbled something else then said clearly, "Where? State and Madison, okay. I'll get right over."

Again he hung up and pushed the telephone across the desk to Manny Roberts. "Didn't take long, did it," he said pleasantly.

"Yeah, thanks," Roberts told him. "We didn't even know it was out. We 'preciate you boys on a night like this. Thanks again."

Bolan was putting away his tools. Joliet Jake growled, "Thanks, hell. Give the boy a double-saw."

Manny sprang to do so.

Bolan accepted the bill and stuffed it into a pocket.

"Thanks," he said, and quietly withdrew from the enemy camp, past the hordes of bored warriors, and back into the friendly storm.

9: ODD MAN OUT

Steely nerves and a sharp application of derring-do had accompanied that hazardous penetration of enemy territory, to be sure; but Bolan had more going for him than sheer audacity. He had learned in the school of harsh necessity that the human mechanism "sees" with more than the eyes. "Seeing" is a concerted mental activity consisting of a matching-up of retina-image with the mental storehouse of past experiences, as superimposed upon the awareness-needs and desires of the moment.

Bolan would perhaps not describe the process in just this manner, nevertheless he thoroughly understood the human mechanics involved and habitually made full use of this natural condition. Long before the Mafia wars he had become a consummate and instinctive actor in the masquerades he called "role camouflage."

Once, cut off and trapped inside enemy country in Vietnam, Bolan had draped a standard black poncho about his shoulders, donned a straw coolie hat, and knelt in the open over a fishing net in a narrow stream for two hours and in broad daylight while enemy soldiers searched all about him. Despite his relatively great size and the makeshift nature of his "costume," the image reflected in the searchers' eyes and as interpreted by their perceptive processes was that of a black-pajama-clad villager tending his nets—and this, of course, was not the object of the frantic search.

Similarly, in the penetration of *Manny's Posh*, the enemy had been set-up—by the storm (past experience) and by Bolan's own purposeful machinations (present awareness-needs)—to accept in their midst the presence of a telephone lineman. It is doubtful that any person in that club could have later provided any sort of valid description of "the guy who came to fix the phones"—except that "he was done up for th' South Pole."

Bolan's understanding of the enemy and his own remarkable self control played a heavy part in the success of such ventures, of course. Also, it seems, an appreciation of subtle situation-humor rode with him into the danger zones. Note, in this particular application, the meaningless double-talk about "flux fields."

The incursion into *Manny's Posh* had meant considerably more to Bolan than a routine combat recon. He had been interested in finding a weak spot in the enemy's armor. Joliet Jake Vecci, overlord of the lucrative and therefore highly-prized downtown territory, emerged as the most likely target. An underboss, or *subcapo,* in the Chicago syndicate for many years, the aging Vecci had for some time been quietly agitating for "a kick upstairs" to the honorary status of co-*Capo,* or *Capo Emeritus* of the Chicago Family. This could and would have been accomplished but for Vecci's insistence upon retaining direct reins of power in his old territory, a desire which produced considerable friction and displeasure among the younger ranking members of the organization.

106

Friction, intrigue, and ruthless competition were, of course, no strangers in the supposedly closeknit Cosa Nostra families—and a crafty old powerplant like Jake Vecci was not unaware of the restless maneuverings about him.

This was but one of the interesting stories to emerge from Leopold Stein's notebook, but it seemed to Bolan to be one of the best exploitable at the moment and under the circumstances of the night. Thus, the search for Vecci had been no routine probe but an important combat mission.

And it had required no great feat of imagination to pinpoint this Mafia gathering in the heart of Vecci's territory. Simple observation and alertness had led Bolan to the accurate conclusion that "the boys are mobbing up" at *Manny's Posh*. The logical extension of this discovery called for a soft probe of the club. This Bolan did, very effectively, and he came out much the wiser and with another "inner ear" direction to his battle plan.

He had instantly recognized Joliet Jake and guessed the identities of Meninghetti and Spanno. The man in the gray suit posed the only mystery, but he had obviously been subservient to Vecci and therefore occupied little of Bolan's mind. The important thing was that he had located the weak spot he'd sought, and it was time to strike.

Bolan left the war-wagon on a side street just around the corner and returned to the alleyway on foot. He ascended a telephone pole behind the building housing *Manny's Posh* and swung onto the roof. On a previous visit he had run two splices from that pole—one giving him direct access into the main trunk line serving the neighborhood, the other into the private line to Man-

107

ny's office. Now, he clamped into the main trunk and used his lineman's phone to call the number in that office just below.

The voice of Manny Roberts responded to the first ring with, "Yeah."

In his best Executioner tones, Bolan said, "Let me speak to Jake."

"Who's this?"

"Never mind who. Just put Jake on."

The muffled, off-angle voice announced, "Some guy, won't say who, wants to talk to you."

Bolan heard a peevish "Awright" in the background. He settled himself against the sheltering lee of the parapet and waited, visualizing Manny Roberts hurrying the telephone over to the old man. Then the rasping voice was strong in the receiver. "Yeah, who's there?"

Bolan said coldly, "I wanted to make sure you were out of the way."

"What's that? Who the hell is this?"

"Shut up and listen, and get it straight the first time through because I'm not repeating it. I'm taking this town out clean, Jake, and I want you clear. You stay where you're at."

"I don't—who the hell is this?"

"Do I have to spell my name in black, dammit?"

Bolan heard heavy breathing and nothing else for a moment, then: "This's no time for games. If you're who I think you are, why're you calling *me*? Why the friendly warning?"

"I didn't say it was friendly," Bolan replied. "It's just that you won the odd-man-out toss. I'm letting you survive, Jake, only because I'll know who to keep an eye on in the future. I know there'll be plenty of scum left behind when I blow this heap. And I've elected you king of the leftover scum."

The underboss was moving quickly toward apoplexy. He cried, "Hey who is this? Is this—hey it's no time for practical jokes!"

"It's no joke. Count your blessings and light a case of candles when you go to bed tonight, 'cause you'll be the only boss left. But you stay put right there. I'm hitting, and soon, so you stay clear."

Bolan broke the connection and immediately moved his patch to the office line. He expected that Joliet Jake would be making a call of his own, and soon. Bolan wanted to be in on it.

He waited in the stiff cold for two minutes . . . three . . . four—then the receiver down below was lifted. Bolan heard harsh breathing and the coded beeps of the touch-tone dial system. He recorded the combination while the connection was being made, then he listened quietly to the hushed conversation.

"This is Jake. Is he there?"

"Uh . . . just a minute."

"Yeah, hello."

"Hi, how's it going?"

"So far so good. How with you?"

"Not so good. I think the bastard just called me."

"He *called* you? He called you *there*? At—"

"Yeah, where I told you I'd be. Who else did you tell I'd be here?"

"Why would I tell anybody? I didn't tell anybody."

"Well . . . I guess I got to believe it was him. Or else someone's getting awful damn cute with the old man."

"Maybe he's been watching you. He could've followed you there."

"Or else we got a loud canary somewheres close by."

"That guy is—well what'd he want? What'd he call you for?"

"He says he's getting ready to wipe everybody out. Everybody but me."

A nervous chuckle greeted this disclosure. "Damn big of him, isn't it. What's this love affair with you?"

"Ahhh, some screwy . . . I'll tell you all about it later. The thing is, I thought I better pass the word around. I mean in case this guy has some kind of inside line. It makes me nervous as hell, him glomming right onto me like that. I almost have to believe there's a canary somewheres. *If* that was really him. And if it *wasn't* him, then maybe I'm even nervouser. You know what I mean."

"Yeah." This other voice was taking on a decidedly different quality. "I know what you mean. You could be right about that canary, too. In that case, it's probably someone right there in your own outfit."

"I know, that's what worries me too. Listen, what do you think? Should I call the others?"

A pause, then: "Hell, I can't advise you on anything like this. It's your outfit, not mine."

"Sure but you know how I always valued your advice."

"Well . . . I don't know. If it was me, I guess I wouldn't tell anybody. It might be misunderstood. Besides, this boy is plenty tricky. He could be just setting you up."

"You think so?"

"Sure, it could be. Listen, here's what I'd do. Get ahold of Larry Turk. Put him on it. That way it's out of your hands. Then just sit tight."

"Yeah I guess—hell, I can't get ahold of Turk. He's

taking the Hauler to a carpet."

"Already?"

"Hell yes. He says it has to be settled right now tonight. Says he either has the authority or he doesn't. And he's not taking any responsibility for another Acres until he knows exactly where he stands."

"You know what that means for Pete, then."

"Yeah. Well, I guess he deserves it, eh? Listen, I can't just sit here. That bastard might bomb the place or set it on fire or something. You know how he is."

"Yeah I—hey! Did you search that place for bugs?"

"Hell yes we tore the joint apart. I got suspicious for a minute—a guy came in awhile ago to fix the phones. Storm knocked the lines down or something. But he didn't plant nothing, I'm sure of that now."

"Well . . . okay. Listen, where are they holding that carpet on Pete?"

"Out at—you know."

"Okay, here's what I'd do. I'd give a call out there and try to catch Turk. Just tell 'im you're checking in about this latest thing. Tell him all about it. It's his job to think of something, isn't it? Let *him* decide what to do, and it'll also prove that you're on the right side."

"Whattaya mean, prove I'm on the—?"

"Now hold your horses. Hell I didn't say *I* thought anything like that."

"Anything like *what*, f'Christ's sake!"

"You know what I mean, this boy calling you direct and all that. With this old trouble, somebody might get the wrong idea."

"Well somebody just better not!"

"They just might, anyway. Call Turk, Jake. Put it on him."

A brief silence, then: "I guess you're right. Okay,

thanks. Are you staying right there?"

"Well, uh, yeah I might."

"Whattaya mean, yeah uh you might! What kind of answer is that? Are you afraid to tell me where you're gonna be?"

"Hell, you know better."

"Awright, then, just what are you telling me?"

A pause, then: "I'm not telling you a damn thing, Jake."

A click signaled the end of the connection. Bolan grinned, listening to Joliet Jake's dazed, "Well can you beat that?" as he hung up at his end.

The wait for the next call was much briefer. Again Bolan recorded the touch-tone combination, but it quickly became a useless piece of pre-intelligence as a smooth voice announced, "Giovanni's."

Joliet Jake's trouble tones crowded the line. "This is Mr. Vecci. I'm—uh—interested in a private party you got going there. You know the one I mean?"

"It's all private tonight, Mr. Vecci. We're hard."

Bolan raised his eyebrows. "Hard" meant that mob figures only were present at Giovanni's, an exclusive nitery in the suburbs, even to the waiters and bartenders and kitchen help.

"All right, that's swell. Listen, who's this?"

"This is Charles Drago, Mr. Vecci. What can I do?"

"You can collar a certain someone and get 'im to the phone for me, Charlie. He's bringing somebody there to a carpet."

"Oh, well they haven't arrived yet, Mr. Vecci."

"Christ they should've been there long ago."

"I guess it's the storm, sir. It's delaying everybody."

"Well dammit."

"In the meantime, Mr. Vecci, you can channel reports for him through—"

"I'm not channeling no *reports*," the underboss growled.

"I'm sorry, Mr. Vecci, my tongue tripped. I was just trying to be—"

"I know, helpful. Okay, Charlie, here's how you can be helpful. You watch that door like a hawk. The minute he comes in, you tell 'im to call me at Manny's."

"Yes sir, at Manny's."

"Right, and don't tell nobody else. And tell him it is urgent," Vecci added, spacing the words for emphasis.

"He'll get the message, Mr. Vecci. And nobody else."

"Okay thanks."

This time it was Joliet Jake who broke the connection. Bolan moved his patch to the trunk line and scanned the Stein Intelligence with a pencil flash. On the fourth page he located the telephone number which corresponded to the coded beeps of Vecci's first call, and his lips pursed thoughtfully as he noted the name opposite that number.

Bolan pondered for a moment, then placed his second call of the mission. The same voice that had answered Vecci's earlier ring said, "Yeah."

Bolan asked, "Is he there?"

"No he's not here."

"I know damn well he is. Put him on."

"He—uh . . . who's calling?"

"Never mind who's calling. Put him on, and damn quick."

"He—uh—isn't taking no more calls tonight."

"He damn well better take this one," Bolan growled.

"Well . . . just a minute."

Presently the other voice came on the line, cautious,

113

reserved. "Okay, what's all the fuss?"

"Listen, they want you to get it out to Giovanni's, and right away."

"They who? I'm afraid you have the wrong number."

"Have it your own way," Bolan replied coldly. "You got the message, that's all I got to tell them."

"Wait a minute. I don't recognize your voice."

"Maybe you're not supposed to. And maybe you better get it out to the suburbs, and quick."

"In this storm? They know I don't go—"

"You better go for this one. The cards are being cut, and you better be ready to pick a side."

The guy was getting flustered. Obviously he was not accustomed to being talked to in this manner. He wheezed, "I don't—well now wait a minute. You'd better tell me what's up. I'm not going anywhere unless I—"

Bolan clipped off the protest with, "Just a minute." He held a hand over the transmitter, counted to ten, then came back in a warmer tone of voice. "They said tell you it's for your own good, and thinking of the future. A vote is going to be taken, maybe for a contract or something, and they suggest that you keep that quiet."

"Does this have to do with that carpet for Pete the—?"

"No, they wouldn't ask you out there just for that. I told you it's a new deal. A certain old man seems to be going off his rocker, and they're taking a vote for his retirement. Now I already told you too damn much. You keep this quiet."

"Oh sure, I understand. Well what—I mean, I don't have any vote."

"They say you got an interest, you should at least want to be here when it's all decided. If only to show

114

where you stand. Uh, like I said. There's liable to be a contract or two made out."

"Well . . . okay, thanks. Tell them I'll try to make it. If I can get through this weather. Uh, about how much time do I have?"

"Not much. Most everybody's already there."

"Okay, thanks again. Tell them I appreciate it."

The line clicked and the dial tone hummed in Bolan's ear. He smiled wryly, shifted his position to unkink his muscles, and promptly patched back into Manny Roberts' private line. He got there as the phone was ringing and waited patiently for the conversation he expected to take place. It did.

"Yeah, hi."

"Hi Jake. Listen, I just heard something terrible. This is for old time's sake. Something's going on up at Giovanni's."

"Yeah I know, they got a thing going there. On Bolan I guess. What d'ya mean, old times sake?"

"I mean I can't even be seen looking out a window at you. You get what I mean. Stay away from that thing at Giovanni's. It's not what you think. Forget about Turk, don't let them even know where you are. Lay low."

"What the hell are you . . . ?"

"That's all I can say, Jake. I'm sorry, really sorry as hell."

Again, "City Jim" hung up on the underboss, and again Bolan heard the post-connection muttering of the bedeviled old man below: "What th' hell is goin' on around here?"

Bolan severed his patches, gathered his gear, and muttered into the teeth of the storm, "It's the name of the game, Jake. Odd man out. And you're all the oddest bunch I ever saw."

10: A CALL TO BATTLE

Bolan made the final telephone probe of the series from a public booth on the near North Side. A smooth voice answered with the standard announcement: "Giovanni's."

Bolan put his voice in the streets and asked, "Listen, is this Charlie Drago?"

"Sure is, who's this?"

"This is—uh just call me Phil from Jersey. Listen, Mr. Drago, I was referred to you. I got something I don't know what the hell to do with. I was told maybe you're the right man to put it on."

"Who'd you say this is?"

"Just say it's Phil from Jersey. I'm just passing through, I don't live around here. But listen, I'm down in this bar, this joint on South State, and I hear this strange conversation in this next booth to me, see. And I—"

"Well now wait a minute. I got no time to be—"

"You better take time, Mr. Drago, if you'll pardon me. This is red hot stuff and I ain't asking for nothing in return."

Grudgingly, but with apparently growing interest,

Drago replied, "Okay, what's this red hot stuff? Make it quick, eh?"

"These guys are talking about Bolan, this Mack Bolan creep. Listen, I know all about that creep. And one of them is saying it's sure funny how things're working out, with this Bolan turning out to be their best buddy. Naturally I keep on listening."

Drago interrupted the recital with a hurried, "Just a minute, Phil. I want to get somebody else in on this, too."

Bolan lapsed into silence, lit a cigarette, waited for a full two minutes, then he heard another telephone open onto the line and Drago's smooth tones told him, "Okay, Phil. Pick up where you left off."

"Where was I?"

"You're in this bar on South State and these boys are saying that things are working out now with Bolan their best friend. Take it from there."

"Okay, and I really perk up when I hear this. I'm afraid to look around the partition, I just freeze there with my head against the booth and I keep listening. This one boy is saying how they just been waiting for something like this, and I get he means the Bolan thing. Then I start getting a whole different idea when this other boy comes in with something about how he still can't figure the old man and Bolan cozying it. Well that put a whole different picture together, didn't it?"

"What old man?" asked a second voice from Giovanni's.

"I don't know, sir. That's just the way they mentioned him every time, just the old man. Anyway this other guy comes back with it's a good thing, 'cause the old man is about getting ready for an open war anyway. I get it

118

right away these boys are talking up a street war, mixed up somehow with the Bolan thing."

"Is this all you heard?" Drago asked calmly.

"Naw, I also got it that this old man has got this hundred or so soldiers meeting at another joint somewheres around there. Let's see, Minnie's place or something I think."

"I never heard of no Minnie's place," declared the sscond voice.

"That's what it sounded like. Minnie's or something like that."

"How about Manny's?"

"Well, yeah, I guess it could've been that."

"God dammit," declared a totally new voice.

"How many boys did you say were meeting there?" asked the second.

Bolan/Phil-from-Jersey replied, "That's just how they said it, a hundred or so soldiers. Now I can't put this rest in no exact words, I mean you know how it is, a lot of grunting and hum-hawing around, and like you follow the drift but there really ain't that many words."

"Okay," Charles Drago put in. "What was this drift you got?"

"That these boys are gonna be loadin' up and comin' out to your place there, Giovanni's. And I heard something else just funny as hell."

"What's that?"

"One of 'em said something about police cars. I b'lieve they mean to make it look like a bust, you know?"

"God dammit," said the third voice.

"Wait, just wait," the second man drawled. "Let's sort this all out. Who is this giving us this story?"

119

"Phil from Jersey is all you got to know. I don't want to wind up in the middle of no local war. I'm just passing along what I heard. You'll have to take it from there."

"Are you one of us?" the man asked the "informant."

"Sure, I'm with—well, I'm familied-up in Jersey. That's all I want to say about that."

"Okay, we always got along good with our friends in Jersey. Now tell me, Phil—how did these boys think Bolan figured in all this?"

"Like I said, it sounded to me like he was mobbing up with them. Course, that sounds pretty far out. Maybe I got it wrong. Maybe they're just using the creep as a smokescreen. You know."

"Yeah I know, Phil. Okay. Listen, we won't forget this. When the dust settles, you look me up. Okay?"

"I guess I don't know who I'm talkin' to."

"You just ask around for Benny Rocco."

Bolan's eyebrows lifted. Rocco was an up and coming big man in the North Chicago territory. The Executioner told the up-and-comer, "Okay, Mr. Rocco, I'll sure look you up first chance I get. Uh, Mr. Drago—are you still there?"

"Sure, I'm here."

"Okay, I guess that's all I know. I can't remember this boy's name that put me on you. But he said you'd want to know, and I figured you had a right to."

"You did right, Phil. And you'll never regret it. Give our regards to our friends in Jersey, eh?"

Bolan said, "You bet," and hung up.

He dropped his cigarette into the snow and hurried back to the war-wagon. The night was beginning to shape up now. And he did not wish to miss a minute of it.

The "back office" at Giovanni's in any brief comparison's with Manny's Posh would present the latter as an outhouse on a baronial estate. Heavily carpeted floors and panelled walls, a magnificent built-in bar and stereophonic sound system, original oil paintings, long and graceful leather lounges and heavily padded chairs, and even an adjoining powder room; a one-way window covering an entire wall and allowing an unrestricted view of the main clubroom—these were but the most notable features of this fabulous "office."

Arturo (Don Gio) Giovanni would proudly display to the most casual visitor the quieter but equally sumptuous details of this boyhood dream come true—such as the massive teakwood desk, handcrafted and flown in from Singapore; door, window, and even drapery remote-controllers built into the fantastic executive chair which was also fully automated and wired for sound and vibration; the sun and sauna terrace and massage room; and many miscellaneous fine appointments which made this truly "an office fit for a king."

And, of course, Giovanni deserved this office—he was the King of Chicago and diverse points east, south, north, and west. The imperialistic stretch reached into such unlikely places as Texas and Arkansas, to Florida and into the Caribbean, to Europe and even to Hawaii. Certainly no king, of any time or place, enjoyed more raw power and accessible wealth than this former Neopolitan street urchin turned American at the age of eight, reform-school veteran at fourteen, bagman and bodyguard and torpedo during the rough and rowdy pre-Capone Chicago of the twenties—and now undisputed boss of an empire with an annual take in excess of two billion dollars.

This seemingly benign old gentleman, so proud of this lavishly ostentatious office in which he spent perhaps eight hours per year and a criminal record spanning nearly fifty years, with a list of arrests covering six closely-spaced typewritten pages and on every charge from intimidation to mugging and murder, conspiracy, bribery, rape, simple assault, assault with intent, bookmaking, counterfeiting, bootlegging, and everything that could be worked into a busy lifetime of crime. In appearances before various crime committees, Giovanni had taken refuge under the fifth amendment for a grand total of one hundred and thirty-seven times. With all of this, however, Don Gio had been convicted of but two crimes since his fourteenth year, and both of these convictions were later reversed by friendly appeals judges.

Talk had been going around lately that the *capo* was getting soft with age, that he spent too much time pampering himself in places like Nassau and Rio and Honolulu, that he had so many personal "legit" financial interests now that he wasn't too inclined toward the nitty-gritty of syndicate management—and most of this kind of talk had been coming out of the downtown territories ruled by Joliet Jake Vecci.

Apprised of this loose talk by concerned court attendants, Giovanni usually waved it off with a chuckle; he would point out that Nixon had his winter whitehouse, his western whitehouse, his summer and spring and fall whitehouses—why the hell shouldn't Don Gio have his places to get away from the pressures sometimes. As for personal financial interests, what the hell was he supposed to do with all his money, sit and look at it? Hell no, he put it out to work for itself, and with enough spreading around to give the tax boys crying fits, and these other Chicago boys could learn something from the *Don's* example if they'd listen more and cry less. *Crime* might some day start listening to all the nasty things being said about it, and it might stop paying, after all.

And Don Gio would laugh and step into his gold-trimmed limousine or his private Boeing 727 and go off somewhere to forget the pressures and the damn FBI guys falling all over him everywhere he went and writing down what he ate and if he grunted or burped.

On this particular night, however, the *Capo* was not laughing. The time had come to face a pressure or two head-on.

First off, this Bolan punk. The kid had been allowed to run too high, wide and handsome for too damn long, and it was about time someone shoved a cold bar up his rear and lowered him slowly into one of those blast furnaces down at East Chicago.

Secondly, there was this matter of shameful insubordination and maybe even open rebellion within the family ranks. When high-ranking and responsible officers starting running around and assing it up like common street soldiers, then something was certainly going very sour with the organization. Gio would have to make an example of this latest trespass, even though things went way back between the *Capo* and this old buddy from the street days under Capone, this Pietro Lavallo whom Gio in the old days always called *Golden Peter* because he always had such luck with the girls. So now this little Golden Peter was the magnificent fuckup, Pete the Hauler, and old times never paid the way for new ones. Pete Lavallo would have to pay his own way now; it was the price of manhood in a disciplined society.

And now this latest blow, the exclamation point for this matter of family discipline. Sure, the *Don* had known for a long time that his old pal Jake had been agitating for something. But *this*? And at such a time?

The *Capo* scowled and drummed his fingers on the polished teakwood surface of his Chinese desk and tried to read the minds of these three young men standing here and telling him about a street war right within the family. Did they really believe it theirselves? Were they hoping their information was good—or bad? Was everybody looking for their *Don* to step down and place the mantle of power on younger shoulders? Were they looking for a shoot-out between the oldsters, and a whole new deal?

This tough Larry Turk was telling him, "There is a Phil Tarrantino with our friends in Jersey, Mr. Giovanni. He was made by way of Danno Giliamo, and in fact he was with Danno in England on that Bolan hunt over there. He got hurt during that, Danno tells me, and he's been just sort of recuperating and taking it easy. Danno last saw him on Monday—he said he was drifting toward Vegas. Maybe some light action in the heat out there might help him get back on his feet.

"So I don't know, Mr. Giovanni—I can't locate no handle on the boy in Vegas. It could be that he just drifted this far, and got stuck by the storm and is just waiting a chance to move on. I'd say—"

"When we're in this office here," the *Capo* instructed kindly, "you can call me Gio. All of you. Okay? It sounds better."

124

"Sure, Gio."

"I wish you'd brought this boy out here so I could talk to him myself personal. I like to hear it right from the horse's mouth."

Benny Rocco shifted about nervously and admitted, "I made that decision, Gio, and I'm sorry you don't like it. The boy was nervous as hell and I could tell that he would blow right out if I started pressuring him. I wanted to keep him friendly."

"Well, maybe you handled it right after all, Benny," Giovanni replied. "At least . . ." The steely gaze shifted to Charles Drago, the chief doorman and undeclared security boss during the club's normal operations. "At least I got to say Charlie used his head, getting more than one witness to what was being told."

Drago smiled soberly and said, "Thanks, Gio. I don't know why, I just didn't think you'd want to be bothered with—I mean, it didn't seem that important at the time. You know how this stuff goes around. I figured it was just some more of that gossip always drifting up from the Loop."

"Yeah," Giovanni replied sourly.

"That stuff about the police cars is what turned me around," Rocco stated quietly.

"Yeah," the *Don* agreed, slipping even deeper into the thronelike chair. "With good cause. Jake has more personal clout than even I got. I should've took him off that territory a long time ago, I guess. The way him and City Jim have been cozying it up these past few years . . . I guess . . . well, so you boys think it's straight stuff, eh? Turk? You're willing to risk everything you've built up on the strength of what this will of the wisp from Jersey told you with miles of phone wires between you?"

"It checks out, Gio," Turk assured his *Capo*. "I sent

125

two boys around there, my own personal boys, to really look it over. Jake has got about a hundred boys all right, mobbed up at Manny's. None of 'em even knew what they were doing there, except they were told they're going to be riding in police cars. Then these crew chiefs came out of the office and threw my boys out. I mean flat tossed their asses out in the snow."

"That's a carpet offense right there," Rocco muttered, adding, "They're cooking something, I'd bet my life on that, Gio."

Drago put in, "Jake was sure anxious to have a cozy talk with Turk, I know that much. And he sure put the soft pressure on me to keep it to myself."

"You're saying that he was trying to recruit Turk," Giovanni observed.

"It sure would make a person think so, the way he was quieting it around."

"That just shows how crazy he really is," Turk muttered.

"Well I guess I don't like it at all," the boss declared, scowling even harder. "I just can't picture Jake coming all out that way. Sly stuff, yeah, maybe I could picture that. But this coming all out . . . even to joining up with or recruiting Bolan . . . I can't see Jake doing that."

"If you'll pardon me, Gio," said Rocco, "it does sound pretty sly to me. If he's moving in under cover of this Bolan thing, and maybe even using this boy to run interference for him, then I'd have to say that was a pretty rotten trick."

"Yeah you're right there, Benny," the *Capo* mused. His gaze shifted to Larry Turk. "I proposed you, Turk, you know that—for this thing you've got now."

"Yessir, and I appreciate the honor, you can believe that."

"I didn't do it for honors. I told the council you are the only man for the job. And I sincerely believe that."

"Thanks, Gio. I won't let you down."

"I know you won't. Now . . . about this other matter. Pete the Hauler. Of course, we're not supposed to discuss this beforehand. But . . . well, you understand, this is a really unusual thing we got going here tonight, I mean all of it together." He drummed his fingers on the desk top for a moment of quiet thought, then he sighed and said, "Light me a cigar, Charlie."

In misery, Turk thought, *Well here's where Pete the Hauler gets let off.*

Drago had produced a silver cigar holder and carefully placed in it a roll of leaves that were valued at approximately $50, considering the expense of having a box specially flown up each week from Jamaica. He lit the cigar, then removed it from the holder and passed it to the *Capo*. The silver holder went back into Drago's pocket and the *Capo* went on with his "forbidden discussion" with Larry Turk.

"But listen now, Turk. I know that what happened down there this evening between you and Pete is just like you claim. I know that, mainly because I know *you*, and especially because I know Golden Peter Lavallo. He and Louis were about the next thing to asshole buddies . . . I've even wondered about those two sometimes. Well, anyway, I can understand how he could go off his rocker that way and want a piece of Louis' assassin for himself. I mean, you just naturally understand these things."

Here it comes, thought Larry Turk.

"Understanding is one thing, of course," the *Capo* quietly went on. "Discipline is something else again. You know, with all respects to the dead, I never much

127

liked Louis Aurielli. I went along with him mainly for Pete's sake. I'm telling you this so you'll understand what I'm going to say next. Pete Lavallo and me go back a long ways. And I love that boy, I really love 'im. But I love this thing we got, all of us, a whole lot more. And because of that, I'm going to send Pete back down the ladder. I'm going to take away everything he's got. Can you understand that? Everything. I'm going to strip him bare, and I'm going to exile him. I think I'll send him to Arizona or maybe New Mexico. And if he can behave himself out there for a year or two, I'll let him come back. But he'll come back just as stripped as he was when he left. Now that's what I'm going to do to Golden Peter Lavallo."

The three younger men standing at the desk were obviously highly impressed by this kingly predisposition of a pending case.

Larry Turk fidgeted and commented, "I really didn't mean he should get hit that hard, Gio. I just wanted it understood that I couldn't stand for that kind of stuff, not when I'm supposed to be running a thing."

"You boys sit down," Don Gio commanded, suddenly aware that they'd been standing there for quite some time.

The three exchanged glances with each other and pulled up chairs in a semi-circular lineup in front of the desk. Giovanni puffed on the cigar and stared at the ceiling for perhaps a full minute, then the eyes dropped and found their level with Larry Turk's troubled gaze.

"Why do you think I'm telling you all this, Turk?" the *Capo* asked. "And with these other two boys right here listening in. Why do you think?"

Turk didn't have to think. He *knew*. The thing was

almost ceremonial—something pretty great was being conferred here tonight. He hesitated slightly, then replied, "I guess you're showing us your love for this thing of ours, Gio."

"That's right, that's part of it. I don't love it this much, though, just because I'm the boss. It's the other way around. I'm the boss *because I love our thing this much*. Do you understand what I'm telling you?"

"Yessir, and I appreciate the lesson, I really do."

"Okay, don't mention it. But think about it. You think about it, and when you're done thinking you tell me what all this means to you."

"I guess I can tell you right now, Gio."

"So?"

"So it's a damn shame you have to be part of this dirt that's going on, and I don't like you being a part of it. By your leave, Don Gio, I'm taking full charge of things out here tonight. I don't want your mind bothered with such trash. With these two boys sitting here as witnesses, I'm saying that I take full responsibility for what goes on here at this place—and all over town, for that matter. However it comes out, I'm the one made the decisions."

"So. About what?"

"About everything," Turk declared. "But in particular about Joliet Jake Vecci and his downtown rag-a-tags."

Don Gio promptly left his fully automated throne, walked around the desk, placed his hands upon Larry Turk's shoulders, and kissed him full on the mouth. Then he quietly said, "All right, you boys leave me alone now. And send Pete the Hauler in here."

The three confidants to the throne took a hurried leave, and once they were outside, Larry Turk chuckled nervously and said, "Shit, I hope that's no kiss of death."

"It wasn't," Charles Drago assured him. "I never saw the old man do that before. He was genuinely moved, Turk. He really was."

"Well I didn't mean that part," Turk replied. "I mean, if we win, sure, it's going to be beautiful. But what if we lose? Who's holding this big dirty bag, eh?"

Rocco added, "And what if we win here and lose somewhere else. You know what you just did, Turk. You just offered to take all the blame, in case the nationals decide something ain't exactly straight about all this."

"We'll worry about that when we need to," Turk replied brusquely. "Right now we got a lot of things to do. First we got to pull some people offa that Bolan watch. He's tying down just about all the talent we got. And I guess we're not going to play that game, not with what we know now. And we gotta start contacting people. I'll work the underbosses. Benny, you take over and start working on the *caporegimes* and the freelooting civilians, I mean all of 'em. Charlie, you got the oil—I guess you know what your job is."

Drago grinned and replied, "Okay, I'll start phoning people in Jake's outfit."

"You guys have to know," Turk declared soberly, "I'll always remember you for this."

Humorously, Rocco said, "You don't think we'll ever let you forget. You know, this could go down in history."

"And what about Bolan?" Charles Drago asked darkly.

"*Fuck* Bolan," Larry Turk growled. "That guy is way down on my list of worries right now."

130

The trumpets of destiny were loudly sounding the call to battle, it seemed, and more than one empire had been built upon the ruins of war. The turkeymaker would do well to remember, however, that the world is subject to both wars and rumors of wars—and "that guy" —wherever his place on Larry Turk's list, is something of an expert in both.

11: INSIDE STRAIGHT

The atmosphere in Manny's back room had become almost unbearably dense with smoke from cigars and cigarettes, and there was hardly room left to cram another person inside. Crew chiefs sprawled about on the floor, some sitting with their backs against the wall, others kneeling or squattng on their haunches. They had carefully left a "pacing path" for the boss, however, and the old man was seemingly bent on wearing out the thin carpeting along that route, muttering to himself in monosyllabic Italian and every so often pounding his palm with a fist or slapping the wall above the head of a crew chief. Meninghetti and Spanno sat in straightback chairs and stared glumly into space.

No one was talking; all seemed to be quietly pondering the fates of the night. When the boss "thought"—everybody "thought."

Then Captain Hamilton came in and left the door standing ajar, wrinkling his nose at the stale air. He caught Vecci's eye during a downward pass and demanded, "Well?"

"Well I ain't decided yet!" the underboss snarled.

"You've got to make up your mind, Jake," the

Captain pleaded. "I can't keep those cars circling the neighborhood all night. People are already starting to notice. Either we start loading right now or I've got to send them on without you."

"Since when," Jake coldly wanted to know, "is a kinky Chicago cop, even a fat-ass captain of detectives, so damn sure of living through th' night?"

Hamilton's eyes recoiled and he replied, "Don't threaten me, Jake."

"That's not a threat, it's a promise!" Vecci yelled. "Now shut up and lemme think!"

Hamilton crossed over and edged his rear end onto the desk. Mario Meninghetti caught his eye with a sympathetic smile; Hamilton gave him a sick one in return.

The pacing continued for another minute, then Vecci planted his feet and punched a quivering finger toward the police captain. "I ain't sending my soldiers out on no routine patrols until I find out what the hell is going on around here!"

The cop nodded his head agreeably. "I think you're right, Jake—that's good thinking. So let's cancel the whole thing. What you need is a defense line, not a patrol."

"Shut up! Just shut up! *Mario!*"

Meninghetti looked up quickly. "Yeah, boss?"

"Tell me again. Tell me what he said. Exact words now, *exact!*"

"They said that Charlie Drago is calling around. He's saying the time has come to leave the sinkin' ship. Any boys that make it out there by midnight will be welcomed with open arms. Anyone showing up after that, meaning anyone from the Loop *regime*, had better just keep on going clear outta the state."

"That ain't exactly the way you told me before!" Vecci cried.

"Christ, Jake, I'm not no tape recorder."

"Did they say *any* boys?"

"Yeah, that's what they said."

"*By* midnight?"

"Exactly boss, that's exactly."

"Awright, that's great! That's exactly what we'll do!" Meninghetti scowled. "We'll do what?"

"We'll *all* go out there. We'll get this misunderstanding cleared up. We can make it by midnight." The *subcapo* turned to Captain Hamilton. "Didn't you say it'd stopped snowing?"

Hamilton nodded, obvious relief written all over his face. "But it's still nasty as hell out there, Jake. It's a freezing rain now, not too heavy, but the streets are getting hellish. You'd better get moving right away if you're going to make it by midnight."

Meninghetti growled, "Well now wait a minute, Jake. Are *you* going out there too?"

"Sure I am."

"You'll be walking right into it!" the *caporegime* replied despairingly.

"Maybe I will and maybe I won't." Vecci's mind seemed to be made up. Even his good humor was returning. He winked at Pops Spanno and said, "Go out and tell the boys to get ready. We're loadin' up."

"Loading up in *what*?" Captain Hamilton groaned.

"Stop worrying, we're not riding in your bubble-gum machines, that's for sure. I ain't dumb enough to go rolling in there in police cars. Save about two out, and send the rest of them on, Ham."

"What're we saving two for?"

"Escorts, dammit. You ride the front one, and you

135

move through this town damn quick, you hear?"

Hamilton protested, "Jesus Christ, I can't go running off just—"

"The hell you can't," Vecci calmly told him. "The only thing can stop you is a bullet in the head."

The Captain's face turned a beefy red. He spun about and slammed out of the office.

Joliet Jake grinned and told Meninghetti, "Okay, Mario. Let's get moving. Get those crew wagons around in front. I want 'em out there in five minutes and loadin'."

The crew chiefs were scrambling to their feet. Meninghetti told them, "Come on outside, boys. We'll run through this once over lightly, and let's not make no mistakes." As the men filed out, he turned to his boss and asked him, "Are you going to call ahead?"

"Sure I'm going to call ahead. You think I'm nuts or something? Damn right I'm calling ahead."

"Are we going armed?"

"You kidding? You go with every damn arm you got!"

The *caporegime* frowned and followed his crewchiefs out of the office.

Joliet Jake was already on the phone and punching the number for Giovanni's. It would not be proper to call Don Gio direct, not at a time like this, but Gio would get the word relayed to him. He'd better. There was only one way to straighten out a misunderstanding like this—well, *two* ways—and Jake knew exactly what they were. It would either take soft words or hot lead.

Either way, Jake sure wasn't waiting until half his soldiers had gone over to the other side before he started working toward that understanding. Hell no. Joliet Jake hadn't survived forty years on the streets on *that* kind of dumbness.

A taxicab was idling at the curb in front of Manny's Posh. The meter was ticking and the cabbie was chatting amiably with his fare, a tall man in a gray suit and topcoat. A gray Homburg was worn square across the forehead, a leather patch covered one eye, and an unlit pipe was clamped loosely between his teeth. A small square briefcase sat on the seat beside him.

Another man in gray emerged from the club and stepped in front of the cab to peer agitatedly down the street.

The cabbie told his passenger, "Okay, he must be the one. That's Captain Hamilton out of Central."

The man with the eyepatch murmured his thanks and dropped a twenty dollar bill over the seat as he exited.

Hamilton had moved into the street and was waving down an approaching vehicle, a police cruiser. The cruiser pulled to the curb behind the taxi; Hamilton walked along the street side of the cab, moving with care on the freezing surface, and was intercepted beside the police car by the man with the eyepatch.

"Are these your vehicles, Captain?" the man snapped.

"Who wants to know?" Hamilton replied, eyeing the man warily.

The guy showed him a thin smile and said, "Tell you what, Captain. I won't mention your name if you won't ask mine."

"Okay, what's up?" Hamilton said, sighing.

"Jim has had about a dozen calls about this police parade you've got here. He says, for God's sake, break it up."

"You tell Jim I've been trying to do that for nearly half an hour. And you tell him, furthermore, that something's going to have to be done about that crazy old man in there. I believe he still thinks he's living in the 1950's or something."

"Jake can be hard to take sometimes. But so can a two block lineup of police cars. What's the idea?"

"Aw, that old lunatic got this wild plan for planting torpedoes in police cars and running Bolan to ground. I think he wanted to show the youngbloods around here that the old men still have plenty of the oldtime muscle. Anyway, he thought he was going to personally capture Mack Bolan and proudly display his head on a warpole or something. But I've got him talked out of it. I was just coming out to send the cars away."

"I recommend that you do so without further delay."

"Yeah. Listen, can you get a message to Jim for me?"

"I'll try."

"Jake has gone plumb crazy. He thinks there's a contract let on him or something, and he's going out to Giovanni's now for a showdown. He's taking a big head party, and I've been elected to escort them out there. Tell Jim to for God's sake do what he can to head this off. There's no telling what might happen. All of us might be in for a whole lot of hell."

"You're not escorting him with all these cars, I hope."

"No, he very kindly settled for a two-car escort. Look, I've got to get this moving, so . . ."

"By all means. Do me a favor first. Get me a ride to Central."

"I'll call in a car," the Captain agreed. "Don't forget that message."

"Okay, and listen . . . a word of advice. If things do start going to hell—well, when it gets down to sheer survival remember that first and last you're a cop. Get me?"

"Thanks, I'm learning that fast."

Captain Hamilton leaned into the cruiser and reached for the radio microphone. The man with the eyepatch limped along the sidewalk and took a station at the curb where the taxi had been. Seconds later another cruiser pulled to the curb, the man got in, and the car sped away.

Minutes later the cruiser eased into the "officials" lane of the Central Police Station in Chicago's loop area. The tall man in the gray suit stepped out, thanked the officers, and went quickly up the steps and inside the station. He was exhibiting a barely noticeable limp, the topcoat was draped neatly over one shoulder; he carried the briefcase in one hand, the unlighted pipe in the other. As he threaded his way through the confusion of uniformed policemen and newspapermen crowding the main lobby area, the man with the eyepatch could have been taken for a police official, a lawyer, or simply a businessman on an errand with the law.

The man was, in fact, none of these. He was the most wanted "criminal" in town at the moment—he was Mack Bolan, in another daring exhibition of "role camouflage."

His uncovered eye scanned the building directory in a lightning sweep as he walked casually past and on to the back stairway, then he penetrated deeper, past the bull rooms and along teeming corridors, and into a quieter area of the building until he found the offices he sought.

The plaque on the door read, *Department Liaison*. He entered and walked through a deserted anteroom, inspecting plaques on the three doors opening from there and selecting the one marked, *Mr. McCormick, State*.

Bolan rapped with his knuckles and went inside. A pudgy man of about fifty looked up from a solitaire layout on the desk, showed a visitor a sour smile, and said, "If it's business, you're too late. If it's not, then you're lost."

"Are you Josh McCormick?" Bolan asked quietly.

"That's me. Stuck in town on the worst night of the year. I guess you're not lost, eh."

"You do the liaison work between the department and the state prosecutor's office." It was a statement, not a question.

The man nodded his head, eyes narrowing in a late inspection of his guest. "I'm one of them," he conceded.

Bolan set the briefcase on the corner of the desk, opened it, and withdrew the Stein notebook. "What stuck you, Mr. McCormick?" he asked in a cold voice. "The weather—or your moonlighting job?"

"What is this?" McCormick growled. "Who the hell are you?"

Bolan had turned the pages of the little book and found the notes he sought. He read aloud, in a voice fit for a funeral service, "McCormick, Josh L.—political appointee, special liaison team for the office of police superintendent, representing state prosecutor in policy matters affecting Chicago Police Department." He glanced up from the reading and inquired, "Are you that Josh McCormick?"

"What's that you've got there?" the man snarled. "What do you—?"

Bolan growled, "Shut up," and showed him the Beretta Belle.

The guy turned pale and pressed his hands flat against the top of the desk. "What th' hell is this?" he asked in a hushed voice.

The notes on McCormick were jotted neatly over six and one half pages of the Stein notes, detailing six years of his close association with known Mafia figures in and out of Chicago, and revealing various details of his treachery to the State of Illinois. He had intervened in scores of criminal cases involving the Chicago syndicate, either buying-off or "clouting" judges and jurists who were not already owned outright by the mob, and often with this influence extending clear into the state supreme court. He had been on the present job for only the past fifteen months, and now functioned chiefly as an informant for his Mafia connections in matters related to their legal wellbeing.

The guy was not a cop, nor an elected official, nor anything other than what the notes indicated. He was a political hack, a paid fink, bagman and clouter for the syndicate—and certainly, in Bolan's mind, he had no more going for him than any fulltime *Mafioso*.

McCormick was breaking out in sweat above the brows and a film was forming over his eyes as he stared up the mouth of the Beretta. He whispered, "I don't know what this is all about. I've done nothing. Is this a contract job? Money? If it's a money job, I'll double the contract, I'll triple it. I'll give you everything I've got."

Bolan's free hand had restored the notebook to its place in the briefcase, and the hand emerged with a marksman's medal. He tossed it on the desk.

It hit the guy's outstretched hand and his eyes focused there, and he gurgled, *"Oh God no!"*

141

Bolan told him, "You've already given everything you had, McCormick. And it's not enough, not nearly enough."

"I'm not Mafia! What does that book say, that I'm Mafia? I'm not, God believe it, I'm not!"

"Maybe you're worse," Bolan told him, remembering Leo Stein's little lecture about the vehicle. "It's people like you, McCormick, that make it all work for them."

"I'm nobody, I'm just a tiny cog in a great big machine, Bolan. Hell, it's not just crime, it's politics, *big* politics. There's a thousand like me, hell maybe ten thousand." The guy was talking for his life, and Bolan didn't even want his life, but he did nothing to discourage the talk.

"Maybe eighty thousand," Bolan said, still remembering.

"I wouldn't be s'prised. It's not little people like me, Bolan. It's the machine, the damned machine. You think *I* have any influence in this town? Me?" The guy laughed bitterly. "I've been in the circles for a long time, sure. I know a lot of people, in the courts and in the police establishment, sure—but do you think I could work anything on my own? They'd laugh me out of town. It's not *me,* Bolan. It's the system, it's the God-*damned* system. A guy can't live around here outside the system; not and make a go of anything."

Bolan knew all about the system. And he knew how easy it was for straight people to get sucked into that mess, and turned into dirt, and remolded like so much clay into the image the system needed.

He told the frightened man, "I don't especially want your life, McCormick. I want your office. I want you out."

"Just give me the chance, you'll see how fast I get out."

"And never come back. You tell it to all your buddies in the system. Tell them that Bolan will be around for a long time, and that he'll be looking into that system regularly."

McCormick was still looking into the Beretta, but there was hope in the eyes now; he was beginning to breathe normally and to settle himself down. He said, "I can't believe that you walked past a thousand cops just to tell me that."

Bolan replied, "You're right, I didn't. Pick up the phone, McCormick. Call your boss in Springfield. I mean your official boss. And I expect you to be very convincing. You've just stumbled onto some solid information. All the celebrities of the Chicago underworld are meeting at Giovanni's at this very moment. They might be talking up a street war. And you have a solid make that Bolan will be crashing this party. And wouldn't it be a neat feat for the state prosecutor if he could very quietly coordinate an army of state and local cops into that little bash out there. That's the idea—now you show me how well you can present it."

McCormick was already placing the call. His hand was shaking but the voice was steady as he told Bolan, "Don't worry, I'm an expert at this stuff, or should I remind you of that?"

Bolan could almost like the guy, even realizing what he was, but realizing also that there were many shades of gray between black and white. He listened critically to the excited two-way conversation, nodded his approval when it was all done, then he tied and gagged the guy and locked him in a closet of the anteroom. That

143

done, Bolan got out of there.

He rounded the corner of the corridor then resumed his affected limping, leisurely making his way back into the swirling chaos that was normal routine for a big city police station—on through scared and snarling suspects, and weeping and angry wives and mothers and sisters.

With a careful disinterest, he pushed on past harried cops and cold-eyed lawyers and cloutmen and fixers of every ilk, through confused complainants and indignant witnesses, on beyond the drunks and the junkies and the frightened kids and the lost souls, on beyond the reporters and the social workers and the photographers, past rattling teletypes and shrilling telephones and back into the frigid but welcome sanity of the wild jungle outside.

And during that trip Bolan quit wondering why sometimes a cop or a lawyer or a judge went sour, or hard, or just plain bad; he had to wonder, instead, how any of them ever kept from it.

He had to wonder, also, if any of this war was really worth it. Was anything actually worth fighting for?

So what if, by some magic and with one mighty thrust of the sword, he should succeed in putting the Mafia down, once and for all, everywhere at once. Wouldn't others arise to replace them, wouldn't the clouters and the grafters and the pushers and the rotten core everywhere simply reassert itself? Wouldn't the shit machine simply reassemble itself?

Hell, he couldn't start thinking like that, he told himself. Doubt must not be allowed to creep in at a time like this. He made his way back to the war-wagon, inspected the heavy-weather tires and double checked the chains, then he stepped inside and changed back into his combat gear.

A very hot war awaited him.

Sure, there was more to life than just taking all you could milk out of it. With so many sucking leeches hanging on, life would sooner or later run out of the good milk, leaving nothing but the bitter for everybody.

Yeah, Bolan had his reason for existence. Sometimes a guy simply felt a hand on his shoulder, and he knew that he was being turned around to look at something rotten, something sucking all the good out of life and leaving nothing but bitterness in its place. According to Stein's notes, more than two-hundred-million bucks a year were being sucked out of the Chicago ghettoes by *the system,* and not a damn cent was finding its way back in.

So bigtime crime created—indirectly—smalltime crimes, juvenile delinquents, broken homes, junkies, and human misery of every description.

This was Bolan's message from Central, as finally broken down and assimilated.

And yeah, that hand was still on his shoulder. Someone had to stop sucking and start putting back in. Sometimes a guy had to be willing to stop and look around him, and maybe volunteer for a transfusion to life.

The Executioner smiled grimly and eased his war-machine onto the icy street.

It was not a war-wagon, he was thinking.

It was a bloodmobile.

12: BATTLE SITE

Bolan's battle plan was simple in conception but delicately complex in its execution. A lone man in a frontal assault could never hope to overcome the staggering array of forces pitted against him; Bolan held no illusions in this respect. He had known from the beginning that the one hope for success lay in his ability to exploit their weakest points, to incite confusion and fear, and to keep the enemy reeling and off balance long enough for the Executioner to take his toll of their leadership.

Jake Vecci, boss of the Loop, had emerged as Bolan's bonus baby, the big wallop of the battle order. Greed and fear, the human factors that had combined to create the *Cosa Nostra,* were now being recombined in Chicago—in only the slightest variation of the original formula—to destroy it. Bolan was the chemist, Chicago was his laboratory, and the most primitive ills of mankind were his materials.

And yes, he just might shake this kingdom down, after all.

The nagging worry in Bolan's mind at the moment, however, was that the larger enemy, the *true* rot that had drawn him magnetically to this troubled old city, actually lay outside the kingdom—that is, outside the

147

family organization itself. Wherever Bolan had gone in the past to battle the syndicate, he had found a condition wherein the mob seemed to be both the cause and the effect of organized evil. This did not appear to be the case at Chicago.

The Stein intelligence bothered Bolan. Oh, the mob was well represented in those notes, okay—they were just as busy in Chicago as anywhere, manipulating and looting and raping their human environment with all the gusto characteristic of *Mafia* entrenchment everywhere.

But . . . Bolan could not shake the growing conviction that the mob's position at Chicago was a unique one. This was a "made" city, yes, but the *Cosa Nostra* had not made it. They were simply a part of the fix and, Bolan suspected, a relatively small part. Actually, it seemed, the city had "made" the mob, not vice versa. The iron grip of power that held this town in virtual slavery did not appear as a typical exercise in Mafia domination. *Mafiosi* were not astute politicians, they did not have the finesse nor even the interest required for the delicate maneuverings that kept a political machine functioning and self-perpetuating.

When the mob really got their hooks into a town, they simply raped it, sucked it dry, and left it writhing in ruin. Like Reading, Pennsylvania, when the Philadelphia mob descended upon it. They bought practically the entire city administration, from the mayor on down, and cowed those they couldn't buy. Before the local citizens could realize what was happening, this quiet heartland of the Pennsylvania Dutch countryside was transformed into the sin mecca of the Atlantic Seaboard, featuring the largest red-light district and the grandest gambling establishment in the East. The most active illegal still since the repeal of Prohibition was operated directly off the city water supply, municipal improvements slowed to a halt, industries began moving out, and the downtown area fell into ruin. The helpless and bewildered citizenry were not even aware of the leeches at their throats until it was too late to save the situation, and Reading was sucked dry before the feds could step in and put an end to the rape.

So why hadn't Chicago been sucked dry, if the mob had truly been in charge here for so many decades? The answer, in Bolan's troubled mind, was that the mob was simply operating a franchise in this town. So okay. Who issued the franchise? Who was the actual "Mr. Big" of this fantastic empire of corruption and clout, an empire which—according to the Stein intelligence—was powerful enough already to dominate *both* political parties in some areas of the state, send handpicked men to Congress and to the legislature and city councils, install federal judges, and even strongly influence the national political organizations and conventions.

Cosa di tutti Cosi, eh? Bolan smiled wryly to himself. It was a mere imitation, a second-generation blueprint. Chicago, it seemed, already had its own version of The Big Thing—and Chicago did not belong to the *Cosa Nostra.*

The Executioner sighed regretfully and shook venal Chicago out of his thoughts. Somewhere he had read that "a people have the government they deserve." Bolan would let the people of Chicago worry about Chicago—and maybe, he decided, people all over the country should start worrying about Chicago. His job was impossible enough as already laid out—and his war was with the Mafia, not with an entire American city and a political way of life.

This shaking-out process helped. A little. It defined

149

the battle-ground and put the enemy in better focus. Bolan did not now "want" The Big Four—he merely wanted the syndicate member of that cartel, "Don Gio" Giovanni. And he had very suddenly lost interest in many of the "nine names" he had requested of Leopold Stein. His guns would be tracking on the hierarchy of the syndicate itself. Let the wage-earning "pigeons" put down their own rotten labor bosses. Let the purchasing-power pigeons put down the gouging businessmen. And let the ballot-marking pigeons handle their own smelly garbage at the polls. All of that was something the people could do for themselves. It was a job for civilians. Bolan had a hot war to fight.

The supper club known as Giovanni's occupied a piece of ground which rightfully belonged to the people of Cook County. Some years earlier the county had acquired, at considerable expense, several sections of unimproved land in this sparsely settled neighborhood for development into a public park and golf course. A particularly choice piece in the northeast corner of this development provided access to the Des Plaines River, and the original park planning called for the construction of a water-recreation facility in that spot.

Through some mysterious reasoning, it was later decided that the water-recreation plan was "unfeasible"—and, by an equally mysterious set of circumstances, the plot of parkland which fronted the river was "acquired" from the county by a recently incorporated firm identified as *Club's Management, Inc.* for the ostensible purpose of constructing and operating a public entertainment facility at that location.

The "public entertainment facility" which emerged was, of course, Giovanni's. No one could complain that the new club was not available to the general public. It was open to anyone who could wangle a table reservation and shell out an average of fifty dollars per head for an evening's entertainment. Patrons were required to observe a strict "dress code" and the joint was "first class" all the way—from the tie-and-tail waiters and headline entertainers in the dining room to the black-tie dealers and table men in the private back room casino.

Just south of Gio's stolen grounds lay the promised but only half-completed (nine holes) public golf course; directly west and across a specially constructed road lay the park proper, covering eight hundred and sixty acres of mostly unusable and therefore unused scrubland. With the river at his back, Don Gio had a rather secluded setting for his night time playground. Only to the north did he have neighbors, a straggling line of upper middle class "estate-ettes" which Don Giovanni contemptuously referred to as "the wealthy man's ghetto"—and which were suitably screened from Giovanni's place by a thick stand of timber.

The club itself was an imposing structure of American colonial architecture which, under standard construction procedures, would have cost perhaps a million dollars to build and outfit. It had not cost Arturo Giovanni nearly so much. Manipulation of building-trades unions and outright ownership of building materials and decorating firms could work economic miracles, and Don Gio was not a man to overlook such important details of smart business procedures. He would pay fifty dollars for a cigar without batting an eyelash, but "give a crummy plumber ten dollars an hour—*never!*"

Yes, it was an imposing joint—and Mack Bolan was

also a man to not overlook important details. The road frontage covered about fifteen hundred feet, bounded by an iron fence and flashily broken at dead-center by an arched gateway and stone gateposts bearing huge coats-of-arms. The county plot-plan showed a triangular-like ground layout, with about three hundred feet of river frontage on the backside of the property. The plot was roughly one thousand feet deep. Bolan estimated the placement of the building at about a five hundred-foot recess into the grounds, reached by an oval-shaped drive from the main road. The joint was ablaze with lights when Bolan arrived on the scene, as were the grounds in certain areas—probably parking lots—flanking to either side.

He would have liked to had a daylight recon of the joint. He knew how deceptive could be the facades of the night, and especially on a night such as this one. The precipitation of the storm front had now degenerated to a light freezing drizzle. Visibility was fair but the ground was a mess of treacherous snow drifts overlain with ice; the roadway itself had incurred very little traffic and evidently no attention whatever from county road crews—not within the past few hours, anyway.

Huddled in a bumper-to-bumper lineup just below the arched entranceway stood a procession of limousines—"crew wagons"—with a Chicago Police Department cruiser in the tail position. Clouds of vapor were rising from twenty or so idling engines and all but the lead vehicle were displaying parking lights; the car in front had headlamps at full blaze. The police cruiser's roof beacon was flashing brilliantly in the falling mist.

Bolan's war-wagon sported a roof flasher, also—the yellow-light type specified for unofficial emergency vehicles. He pulled alongside the cruiser and slid across the seat for a window-consultation with the law.

The door glass of the cruiser descended halfway and Bolan boomed over, "What—is the road out up there?"

"Naw it's all right," was the reply. "Go on by."

"Kinda late at night for a funeral procession, isn't it?"

"Aw, it's just a VIP party for Giovanni's. You know the routine."

Bolan laughed. "Yeah, I know. How 'bout getting an escort for the Edison Company? What a hell of a night, eh?"

"Yeh. I guess the ice is playing hell with the lines, eh?"

The cop was trying to get a better look at the van, which could not have been better disguised by deliberate intent, covered as it was with frozen-on splatterings of dirtied snow from the Chicago streets.

Bolan was replying, "Yeah, and I had to draw no-man's-land out here to patrol. What's up on the other side of this joint here?"

"Damn if I know," the officer told the executioner. "This isn't exactly my beat either."

Bolan chuckled, then said, "Well, I guess I'll find out the hard way," returned to his place behind the wheel, and sent the van into a cautious advance along the line of cars.

The windows of the crew wagons were frosted over on the inside, and only here and there had anyone bothered to wipe away the condensed moisture. But Bolan was head-counting on the basis of normal complements per car—two men in front, two in the jump seats, three in the rear—total seven men including the wheelman times twenty cars—and, yes, it was an impressive force.

The lead car was a crew wagon, not a police cruiser. Bolan speculated that someone, probably one of Vecci's lieutenants, had accompanied Captain Hamilton inside the joint to smooth the way for the grand entry of Vecci's party. And Bolan was thinking that Joliet Jake was behaving much more optimistically than Bolan himself would under similiar circumstances. If there was anything a ranking *Mafioso* feared more than prison or death, it was ambitious competition within his own family group. The mob was forever being rocked from within by unscrupulous maneuverings and greedy intrigue, contrary to all the romantic ideals of solidarity and "brotherhood" espoused by the organization. Any "boss" had earned the name and arrived at that high station by virtue of his own expertise in treachery and double-dealing; he therefore lived in continual suspicion of those around him who had not yet arrived at that level of leadership, and particularly feared those in higher positions who might be inclined to "bring up" someone in direct competition with himself.

So, yes, anyone from the Loop who was crashing that conclave at Giovanni's was on a delicate mission indeed—and Bolan himself was not out here upon any idle business. Not at all. The Executioner had come to join the party . . . and to see that negotiations proceeded favorably.

Favorably, that is, for the Chicago wipe-out.

13: WAR PARTY

Bolan crept on past the Mafia hardsite, stopping twice during the transit to leave the van and let the enemy see him eyeballing the power lines running past the property. During the last such "inspection," a voice called over to him from the darkness beyond the iron fencing: "Hey Mac—watcha doing?"

"Checking the cables," Bolan called back casually. "They're getting pretty heavy with ice."

"Oh, yeah, good idea."

Bolan stood in the middle of the road and lit a cigarette.

"Well, how do they look?"

Bolan told the chatty hardman, "I've seen better. But I guess they'll make it okay if the wind'll just stay down."

"Oh yeah, that could play hell, couldn't it."

Bolan said, "Yeah."

The guy was half-frozen, if the shivers in his voice were any indication. Bolan wondered how many more were patrolling those grounds, and how long they were required to stay out in that frigid weather. It could make a difference in the alertness and efficiency of the defending force; half-frozen warriors weren't worth a hell of a lot.

Casually, Bolan told the guy, "I got some hot coffee in th' truck. You sound like you need some."

"Christ, I'd give ten bucks for some. Make it twenty."

Bolan chuckled and said, "Just a minute," and went into the van. He emerged with a tall thermos and carried it to the fence. The man who stepped out of the night to join him there wore a long black topcoat, a snap-brim hat pulled low, and a wool muffler wrapped about his face. The muffler was frozen stiff and the guy's eyes looked like two burnt holes in a blanket.

Bolan poured the coffee and thrust the little plastic cup through the bars of the fence. The hands which gratefully accepted it were ungloved and stiff with cold.

Sympathetically, Bolan said, "Tough damn night to be out, eh. Are you guarding this joint or something?"

The hardman replied, "Yeah." He sipped the heated stimulant and added, "Christ, you're a life saver. I wasn't kidding. I'll give you twenty bucks for this."

"Forget it," Bolan replied. "Do they make you stand out here all damn night?"

"It's startin' to look that way," the guy chattered. "Uh, you got a heater in that truck, huh?"

"You bet. And I'm wearin' three layers of thermal clothes too."

"What's that thermal?"

"Like insulation. Keeps the body heat in, the cold out. I'm not cold at all, not much, just my face. My face feels like it's dead."

"Well I'm going to tell these boys about that thermal, that sounds like the cat's nuts on a night like this."

"You got other guys standin' around in there freezin' their asses?"

"Yeah. You say your face is dead, listen my ass and

everything that goes with it is dead. I bet I'm shriveled up to a half a inch. I bet if I pissed right now it would spray all inside my stomach."

Bolan laughed and the hardman laughed and a voice from the darkness called out, "Milly, what th' hell're you doing?"

The guy swiveled about and called back, "Just checkin' things out over here."

"Well it's just the power guy. Get on back over here."

The shivering hardman quickly finished the coffee and passed the cup back through the fence. "Thanks," he said. "You'll never know how much I needed that." Then he thrashed off through the snow and disappeared.

Bolan returned to the war-wagon and pondered his new intelligence. They had sentries, and obviously a corporal of the guard who periodically checked them. Those sentires had been out there quite awhile, and were suffering—or at least some of them were. Also, the word had passed quickly along the front about the presence of "the power guy."

Okay, it was enough for starters. Bolan eased the van along until he found the power pole he sought, then he stepped into his munitions lab and began molding a strip of plastic explosive. This he wrapped about his neck and carefully selected two detonators and shoved them into a pocket of the jumpsuit.

Pretty soon everyone in that joint would be made aware of the presence of "the power guy." Yeah, pretty damn soon now.

Captain Hamilton stood silently in the background and kept himself clear of the conversation between Pops Spanno, Charles Drago, and Benny Rocco. It was not a discussion to commit one's self to needlessly.

Spanno was saying, "Now look, Charlie, you're the one calling around and inviting everybody out. Okay, so we come out. Now you're saying . . ."

"It's not Charlie doing the saying," Rocco explained patiently. "Don Gio says it don't look good, havin' all these boys mobbed up out here this way. Charlie meant well when he put out that invite, but hell we already got a couple hundred boys out here, Pops."

"You got that many? I didn't see that many boys out here, Benny."

"You don't have to see them," Drago said. "The point is, Jake knows he's always welcome here, he don't even need an invitation. If he wants to come in, all he has to do is come in. But he's not bringing any hundred boys in here with him, and that's all there is to that."

"Well I dunno," Spanno replied quietly. "I don't think Jake will take it right, being treated like a poor cousin or something. You call around and invite everybody out. So Jake, bein' a good loyal brother, rounds up all the boys and makes sure they accept the invitation. Then when he gets out here, you're saying send all those boys back home. I don't think that's right, and I don't think Jake will take it right."

"I guess he'll have to take it or leave it, Pops," Rocco declared.

"Just who th' hell do you think you're talkin' about, punk?" Spanno said angrily. "That's Jake Vecci sittin' out there inna cold, waitin' to hear that he's welcome to come in with his party. He was a big man in this town when you was nothin' but a gleam in your poppa's eyes."

Larry Turk came in from the outside at just that moment, stamping the snow from his shoes. He growled, "Listen, Spanno. You go tell Jake that if he's scared to come in here by hisself, then he must sure know something that we don't. He can come in any time he likes, but he comes with no more than four cars. That's all. And that's all we're going to say about it."

Turk walked on through the foyer and disappeared around a corner.

"That sounds like the Christ hisself has spoke," Spanno observed drily.

"That's about it, Pops," Drago assured him.

"Okay, I'll go tell Jake. But I can't guarantee how he'll take it."

"I guess we'll just have to run that risk," Drago replied solemnly.

Spanno wheeled angrily about, caught Hamilton's eye, jerked his head toward the door, and went out.

The Captain stepped quietly toward the others and said, "Look, I don't know what's going on, but let's understand something. I'm not part of it."

"We're happy to hear that, Ham," Drago told him.

"I'm out here simply because Jake demanded an escort through town. He was afraid the traffic would be a mess, on account of the storm."

Benny Rocco said, "Well that *is* a head party he's got out there, isn't it?"

"I guess you could call it that," Hamilton replied. "But I don't know what it's all about. Tell Don Gio, eh?"

"We'll tell 'im," Rocco said.

"I'm going back to town," Hamilton pointedly informed them.

"Good idea," Drago declared softly.

"Yeah, uh, thanks. See you boys around."

The Captain took his leave and the two

"youngbloods" grinned at each other and went off to find Larry Turk. Turk would get one hell of a big kick out of this.

Bolan laid in his plastics in a tight coil around the big cable carrying power into Giovanni's, then he emplaced the detonators and returned quickly to the ground. A minute later his war-wagon was plowing along the neglected and largely non-existent river access road which ran through the stand of timber to the north of Giovanni's.

The place had probably been used in years gone by to launch fishing boats into the river. The road simply widened into a turnaround area at the river's edge and plunged right in. Running without lights, Bolan nearly plunged right in with it. The river was frozen-over now and covered with an accumulation of snow.

He stepped out of the van and carefully tested the ice with his own weight, then he went back inside and put on the gray topcoat over his jumpsuit. The Homburg would never do—he passed it by and selected a dark snapbrim and pulled it on at a rakish angle. He checked the Beretta and added another stack of spare clips to the special belt at his waist, then shouldered a Thompson sub and quickly moved out. He sure as hell wanted to be there when the party started.

Quietly Bolan made his way along the frozen surface of the river, hugging close to the shrubbery along the bank. His fingers caressed the little square box at his waist, the miniature radio transmitter which would trigger the detonators on that power line.

Yes, he *had* to be there when the frolic started.

160

In fact, he knew, he would probably have to be there to *start* that party.

Bolan was ready.

Both sides seemed to be ready.

It was about time for the enemy to engage itself.

14: GENTLE BUSINESS

Jake Vecci angrily declared, "Awright, dammit, I'm *going* in! What'd he say, *four* cars? Okay then, you listen. I want ten boys in every damn car, that'll give us forty. I want the best we got, the very best. That means first of all the crew chiefs, all of 'em. Mario, I want you and Pops right at my side. And, remember, the best forty boys we got. The rest waits out here."

"How long do they wait, Jake?" Meninghetti tiredly wanted to know.

"They wait until we get word back to them. Soon as I've got things smoothed out, I'll send the word out here and they can go on back to town. But if they don't get no word in say, half an hour—they better come in theirselves and see what's what. On second thought . . . Pops, maybe you better stay with these outside boys. I don't want to take all the brains inside with me."

"Okay," Spanno agreed, not at all disappointed.

"If you hear anything suspicious going on in there, you come a'running."

"I will, Jake."

"Awright. Mario, you go separate the men from the boys."

Meninghetti took his troubled face away from there and trudged back along the line of vehicles, rousting

163

everyone out into the cold and re-forming the head party into two sections.

Captain Hamilton told Vecci, "Well, I'll be getting back to town."

"What's your big hurry?" the Loop boss sneered. "You afraid of—?"

"That's right, I'm afraid," Hamilton interrupted the tirade. "I have no business out here, the cars from my precinct have no business out here—and in fact, Jake, no man in his right mind has got any business out here tonight. Bolan is probably back there right now just chopping your whole territory into spaghetti. *That's* where you ought to be, not out here on a—"

"Look who's turned into the expert, handing out advice and all, the big bad kinky cop from Central. You make me wanta puke, *Captain* Hamilton. Go on back t'town and count your envelopes. And after you got 'em all counted up, then you sit down and try to remember what you was and what you had before Jake Vecci took you under his wing. Go on, *Captain*, get your dead ass outta here."

Hamilton stifled his rage and flung himself back toward the cruiser. He climbed inside and told the patrolman, "Blow, man blow. And don't look back."

The Captain was already remembering what he'd been before Vecci sprung the fifteen hundred dollars for his first promotion, to Sergeant. He'd been a good honest cop, a guy who slept well at night and could look his kids square in the eyes without flinching. How do you tell a kid that even an honest cop will eventually buy himself a promotion, when that's the only way there is. Yeah, he already remembered. He had never for a moment forgotten.

And as his driver swung the cruiser onto the roadway,

164

during that split second that his headlamps raked the area, Captain Hamilton caught a glint of something in the misty darkness far across the road, over in the park area. Cars—lots of cars, official cars with bubblegum machines on top, moving silently through the darkness with all lights extinguished.

Hamilton whispered to his driver, "Jesus Christ, it's a set! Let's get the hell out of here!"

They got, pausing only for a moment to pass hurried instructions to the cruiser at the end of the procession. But it was to be a short run for the Captain and his two cruisers—less than a half mile—to the State Police barricade which at that very moment was being emplaced across the route of retreat.

Everyone, it seems, had accepted the party invitations.

Bolan was inside the grounds and strolling casually along a beaten path in the snow, the Thompson cradled in his arms.

Someone coughed just ahead. Bolan halted and lit a cigarette, then went on.

A figure materialized in the gloom, a guy with a shotgun, slowly marking time and trying to kick some blood into his feet. Bolan growled, "Hi. Stay with it there, tough."

The sentry coughed again and replied, "What's going on, anyways?"

Bolan told him, "Just keep your eyes open. Joliet Jake and a hundred Loopers are right now standin' just outside."

The guy had obviously wanted to say something else, but Bolan had passed on by without pause. He skirted the brightly lighted portico of the building and went on toward the gate, staying close to the drive. Hardmen were all about the place, leaning against trees, squatting in the snow in groups of four and five and conversing in hushed voices.

Only once was Bolan challenged, by another guy with a chopper who was walking along the drive toward the building.

The hardman said, "Hey, what're you doing up here?"

Bolan pulled the hat lower over his eyes and replied, "Charlie sent me up. He wants to tell you something."

"Charlie Drago?"

"Who else?"

"Well where's he at?"

It sounded very much like the voice that had yanked coffee-loving "Milly" away from Bolan at the fence. Bolan told him, "Just go up to the front door, open it, and look inside. I'll bet that's right where he's at."

The hardman muttered, "Wise guy," and went on toward the building.

Bolan had gone about as far as he wished to go. He was roughly midway between the club and the gate when a pair of headlamps began sweeping in through the arched entranceway. He found a tree with no one lurking about it, got the Thompson ready, and ran his fingers along the radio-detonator box at his waist.

They came in bumper-to-bumper, moving slowly along the oval drive in a leisurely procession. Bolan allowed the lead vehicle to pass his position, then his thumb found the button on the control box.

A hardly noticeable flash from the roadway uprange was accompanied by a muffled popping sound, and Giovanni's was instantly plunged into darkness—club, grounds, everywhere but for that oval drive as illumined

166

by the headlamps of the Vecci vehicles.

The lead car almost stood on its nose in a sudden braking, and the other three plowed into the confused stop at gentle speed but with a horrendous crashing of metal upon metal. Someone over there was cursing with an almost studied precision and all four pairs of headlamps were instantly extinguished.

Bolan cut loose then with the chopper—upon the clubhouse, not upon the procession of vehicles—the heavy weapon sending a withering pattern winging in along the line of cars.

An immediate return fire descended from virtually every direction—not upon Bolan, but upon that stalled lineup of crew wagons.

Car doors were banging and grunting men were flinging themselves this way and that into the snow. Above the roar of gunfire could be heard Jake Vecci's strident screams denouncing the treacherous bastards and exhorting his boys to "kill 'em, goddammit, kill every one of 'em!"

Volleys of gunfire were coming in from the road area now, and men on foot were pounding through the arched gateway and making a run for the little island of marooned vehicles halfway along the clubhouse drive.

Mack Bolan, the life of the party, was quickly fading into the background of action. He had come merely to open the affair, not to conduct it. The Executioner had more important business at hand.

One of the crew chiefs, a man known as Gussie Tate, had been wheeling the Vecci car as they entered that fateful driveway. Mario Meninghetti sat next to the wheelman; Joliet Jake next to him, at the door; seven soldiers in the two seats to the rear.

Vecci had just repeated his instructions to the wheelman to "Take it slow'n easy now, Gussie. Don't make it look like we're roaring in, see. We're coming gently, on gentle business. You gotta keep psychology in mind when you're working this kind of stuff."

Tate had just replied, "Yessir"—and Meninghetti's worried voice was about to make some comment when suddenly all the lights in the clubhouse were extinguished.

Instead of the comment he was working at, Meninghetti cried, "I knew it! Stop the goddam car, *stop it!*"

The loyal lieutenant was already shoving his boss toward the floor when Gussie Tate's heavy foot overreacted on the brake pedal. This action greatly aided Meninghetti's protective reaction—to such an extent, in fact, that Jake Vecci was literally flattened against the floorboards of the limousine. And then the other cars came in like so many derailed boxcars, backlashing the crowded and already unsettled occupants of the lead vehicle.

Joliet Jake was just lifting groggily off the floorboards, his eyes dazed and flaring, when the gutteral chops of the Thompson laced the night.

On this note, Vecci needed no instruction. He was out the door and rolling in the snow and screaming bloody murder, and all of his boys were piling out after him. And then all hell started cutting loose. Gussie Tate fell out of the car with a scream of pain and somebody very close to the sub*capo* began threshing around and turning the snow red with his blood.

Boys were leaping out of cars all along the line and everybody was shooting up the night, and Jake had to wonder if anyone even knew what the hell they were

168

shooting at—Jake sure didn't, and his own snub .38 was in his fist and roaring. He was yelling, "Get in there and wipe out them double-dealing bastards, I mean it! Kill 'em, dammit, kill every one of 'em!"

Then there was a hell of a racket coming from the street, and Vecci knew that Pops Spanno and the Cream of the Loop had joined the battle. He crept away on hands and knees, moving instinctively away from those cars and toward the smell of blood at that darkened clubhouse up ahead.

Jake Vecci, let God be his witness, was going to end a lifelong association with a once dear friend, and he was going to end it damn quick. With God as his witness, Jake Vecci was going to get hisself a *Capo*.

15: WIPEOUT

Don Gio was still talking with Pete the Hauler and four other bosses of the Chicago Council when Larry Turk rapped lightly on the door to the private office and waited for the door-lock release from the inside. The old man's voice came through the intercom instead, with a testy, "What is it now?"

"Larry Turk, Mr. Giovanni. We need a parley, and right now."

The buzzer sounded and Turk let himself in.

Pete Lavallo was glowering from "the hot seat"—a chair placed beside the desk of the big man.

Giovanni told Turk, "We've been giving Pete the bad news and talking over old times, Turk. He agrees completely that a year or two of desert air might do wonders for his sinus. Right, Pete?"

Lavallo growled, "Yeah, that's right"—his eyes not leaving Turk for a moment.

"What I come in to tell you, Mr. Giovanni—this Jake Vecci is outside with about twenty carloads of boys. I told Charlie—"

"I thought you didn't want to smear me up with this dirt, Turk," the old man said quietly.

"Well, no sir, but . . ."

"But you want me to second your motions, eh?"

Giovanni chuckled and turned to Lavallo. "Is your sinus really all that bad, Pete? Do you really think you need this desert thing?"

Lavallo spluttered, "Well I—if you say—what I mean is . . ."

"What d'you think, Turk?" Giovanni asked, still chuckling. "Do you think Pete really deserves all that rest?"

"Like I told you, sir," Turk replied, very softly, "I didn't mean that Pete should get hit so hard."

"Yes, so you said." Giovanni was giving Lavallo the hard gaze. Picking his words very carefully, he told him, "I been thinking—and we got a bad thing on our hands here, Pete. If you'd like to help out—you know—give the young men here the benefit of your years of experience—maybe . . . well, maybe we couldn't spare you for that lazy life on the desert. Huh?"

"Just say the word, Gio," Lavallo replied hopefully. "Anything that suits you is going to suit me also."

"Joliet Jake has lost his mind."

"Is that a fact?" Lavallo had, of course, been aware of the excitement in camp. "That's a bad thing, for a man especially in Jake's position."

"That's exactly what we've been thinking, Pete. He needs to be helped out of it. The young men here haven't had too much experience with insanity in the family, Pete. And I think—and I bet you'll back me up on this—I think an old head like Jake would rather get his help from another old head. Like you. You know? Instead of the indignity of, uh, getting it from one of the youngbloods."

"Yes, I back you up on that a hundred percent, Gio," Lavallo said.

172

The old *Capo*'s eyes moved among the silent group at his desk, taking a wordless poll. Heads nodded and eyes twitched in response to the unspoken question being placed before the council of Jake Vecci's peers. Then Don Gio sighed and told Lavallo, "Well, okay Pete. If you'd like to stay around and give Jake the help he needs . . . then okay . . . I guess we'd have to cancel that desert vacation of yours."

"If that's what you want, Don Gio," Pete the Hauler said solemnly.

"That is what we want, Golden Peter," the old man assured him.

That simply, that quietly, was a contract let and accepted. An invisible death certificate had been drawn upon the atmosphere of that quiet room, and Jake Vecci's name was inscribed upon it with a gentle sigh.

"Well, uh . . ." Lavallo's eyes found Larry Turk. "You say he's outside now?"

"We told him he could bring four cars in," Turk replied. "He might come in, and he might not. Like Mr. Giovanni said, he's lost his marbles. I don't know what he's going to do. But if he tries busting in here with a hundred boys behind him—well, we just can't allow that. There's no telling what he might take it in mind to do."

"No, we couldn't allow that," Lavallo murmured. He got to his feet and told Larry Turk, "I guess I lost my gun back there at that motel. I wonder where I could get one."

Turk produced a small revolver from his pocket and handed it over. "I b'lieve this is yours, Mr. Lavallo," he said.

It was not, but Pete the Hauler replied, "You're right,

it is. Thanks. I guess I better go out and look around. I might bump into Jake and maybe talk some sense into him."

Turk moved to the door with the dazed underboss. He called back, "Sorry to bother you, Don Gio, gentlemen. You won't be disturbed again tonight, I promise you that."

"You see that we're not," Giovanni replied. "We've got important business to go over. What, uh, do you hear on this boy Bolan?"

"Not a thing, sir. He's been quiet as a mouse. I wouldn't be surprised if he's halfway out of the country by now."

"Well I guess we'll see, won't we," the *Capo* replied.

Lavallo and Turk went out, and the door had hardly closed behind them when Lavallo snarled, "Thanks, Turk. Thanks for nothing!"

The lord high enforcer was grinning delightedly. He said, "Hell, all's well that ends well, right?"

"Who says it's ended well?" Lavallo complained. "I ain't done no contract work in fifteen years or more. And I've known Jake Vecci for one hell of a long time. I don't call it ending well. It never had to start."

Turk's grin faded. He growled, "I'm sorry you feel that way, 'specially since Jake is out to get your boss."

Turk had spun away, and Lavallo was replying, "Well now wait a—" When the lights went out.

Turk froze in his tracks, and grunted, "What th' hell?"

"Lights went out," Lavallo informed him.

"Shit, I know that, but I—"

At that instant the peace of the night was broken by the loud rattling of a submachine gun, and this

174

immediately punctuated by the explosive booms of other weapons.

Turk instinctively whirled back to the door to Giovanni's sanctum, then realized that the electric lock and intercom would also be inoperative. He yelled through the door, "Sit tight, Gio, I'll check it out!"

Pete the Hauler was crashing about in the darkness and swearing and vainly clicking a cigarette lighter which was apparently in need of a refueling. "It's that Bolan!" he was yelling. "I knew it, I knew the bastard would show up here! Half out of the country—*bull* shit!"

But Larry Turk thought he knew better. It wasn't Bolan. It was Joliet Jake the Madman and his hundred boys. Somehow they'd cut the power lines and Turk guessed that the war was really on now. And it was just as well. Things had been getting unbearably stagnant in this family. It was time for some new blood at—or near—the top. And Turk had plenty of blood.

As Lavallo threshed about in the darkness, trying to find his way outside, Larry Turk quietly felt his way along the wall and toward the rear. He knew, if he was bent on killing himself a *Capo*, just where he'd be getting set to make his play. And Turk was bent on just the opposite chore. He was going to *save* a *Capo* and thereby assure himself a place in the royal court. Yes, Turk thought he knew exactly where the play would be made.

The human storm had finally arrived, and the thunder and lightning which descended upon the Mafia hardsite was entirely manmade. Rattling volleys, the big booms of shotguns, and the impressive staccatos of big automatic weapons were woven together in a concert of wholesale death that was all too familiar to Bolan's experienced ear.

And this concertmaster was wholly aware of each movement and countermovement, the sounds of command and countercommand, the cries of victory and defeat—and, yes, a very hot war was raging across the holy ground of that blessed thing of theirs. The enemy had engaged itself, and Bolan could think of no better troops to fight this war of liberation; he wished a total victory and a total defeat to each side.

Bolan himself was hardly more than a shadow moving across the field of white, an instinctive creature of the night now, homing on the target of targets for the grand-slam clincher of this mob wipe-out. He gained the rear corner of the building—so carefully noted during his earlier pass—and abandoned the snapbrim hat and overcoat in a snowdrift.

The Thompson went across his shoulders and he began the difficult and dangerous hand-over-hand ascent to the roof, using windowsills and cornices and whatever precarious handhold presenting itself.

The weakened shoulder protested and once threatened to quit altogether, but he issued stern inner commands and pressed on—and then the railing of the private sundeck was his and he was up and over and moving swiftly across the wind-drifted snow of that upper porch.

The French doors gave quickly and with only a light snapping sound to the sudden pressure of Bolan's boot, and he was moving silently across a small room that smelled of liniments and leather and maybe a trace of human sweat lost without labor.

Suddenly the sounds of murmuring voices were rising to meet him, unreal and ghostly against the louder

176

background of the hell let loose outside, and Bolan realized that he was standing at the head of a short circular stairway. Across a metal railing and just below could be seen the silhouettes of several figures standing carefully at a wall and peering obliquely through a window upon the landscape of swirling action outisde.

Bolan swung the Thompson into ready-mode and tossed a small personnel flare toward the center of that room down there. It sizzled into brilliantly flickering patterns of light—and the Executioner knew at once that he had reached the home stand.

The figures at the window—four of them with that prosperous-cheap look of the street hood become boss of all that moved and breathed—whirled about in that awakening which most men find but once in a lifetime. A personal awareness of death-arrived. A weapon flared down there and a chunk of metal tore through the air close enough for Bolan to feel the passage. Already, though, the deadly Thompson was bucking in his grip and he was sweeping that group with a tightly-locked figure-8 burst that flung the entire bunch into the wall and oozing toward the floor.

Another weapon was unloading on him from across the room, and furious chunks of hi-impact stompers were dislodging plaster from the ceiling just above his head. Bolan was working the Thompson in a quick sweep toward that challenge when something hard and heavy crashed into his bad shoulder. The arm fell and the big gun with it, then another blow glanced off the base of his neck and he went tumbling headfirst along the short stairway.

Bolan reached the bottom in a sliding sprawl, fighting to get a hand inside the jumpsuit—but too late. A big guy was slowly descending behind him, pinning Bolan in

the spot of a powerful flashlight, and a big nasty Colt
.45 was peering at him in a way Bolan knew to be
entirely professional.

A breathless voice from across the room, brittle with
age and breathless with the excitement of the moment,
cried, "Save 'im, Turk, save 'im for me!"

"I'm saving him, Don Gio," Larry Turk panted. The
.45 was waggling in a silent command that needed no
words to back it up. Bolan came groggily to his feet and
stood there swaying in the flickering light from the flare,
blinded by the powerful spot in his eyes.

"Hands onna head!" the big guy commanded.

Bolan complied, willing his head to be still and his
mind to find its place. The war was not over yet, he kept
telling himself—he was still alive and functioning.

"Turn around, hands against the wall, feet wide
apart!"

Bolan knew the routine. But he also knew that he was
not going to give up the Beretta without a murmur. "Go
to hell," he snapped.

The old man cackled with delight. "You didn't knock
all the fight out of him yet, Turk. Who is that, is
that . . .?"

"Yessir, it's Bolan," Turk said, the voice edged with
gloating triumph. "Big bad Bolan. We don't want to
knock all the fight out of him at once, do we Gio? A
minute at a time, an hour at a time, we'll just drain it out
of him slow'n easy." To Bolan, he yelled, "Turn to th'
wall, dammit, or do I turn you with a foot in the nuts!"

A new sound of warfare, a somehow different quality
of sound, was rising up in the air out beyond that
window. An amplified voice was carrying across the
grounds and, although Bolan could not make out the
words, that official tone of authority was clear and

unmistakable. He told Turk, "You'd better make your move, turkeymaker. The cops have joined the party."

The old man stepped to the window, taking care to keep his distance from the prisoner, and declared, "He's right, Turk." He stepped back, distastefully eyeing the bloodied dead at his feet, and added, "Look at that, Turk. Look what this rotten bastard did to our friends."

Turk's eyes were beginning to waver and flicker rapidly from side to side. With only the merest telltale trace of nervousness to his voice, he said, "Those cops, Gio. How do we—?"

"Maybe we better turn this boy over to them," Giovanni replied, thinking the words carefully. "For the time being, anyway. It would save a lot of explaining."

"Yeah I—"

A loud commotion was taking place outside the door on the far side of the room. Someone was pounding on the door and an excited voice was yelling, "Open up, lemme in, I got the finky shit!"

Giovanni sighed and declared, "That's Pete the Hauler." His eyes took on a new craftiness and played briefly on Larry Turk. The old man's .45 swung to bear on Bolan and he told his field general, "Go let him in, Turk. I'm getting an idea."

Turk said, "Watch it, I ain't shook him down yet," and reluctantly turned his prisoner over to the *Capo* while he crossed quickly to the door. He fumbled with the override mechanism for the electronic lock and swung the door open.

Pete Lavallo stumbled through, dragging with him a dishevelled and bleeding Joliet Jake, overlord of swinging downtown. At that same moment the lighting in the sanctum flickered and came to life with a dull, yellowish glow.

Turk muttered, "Don't tell me they finally got that generator t'going."

Lavallo, wild-eyed and panting, gasped. "There's cops lining up all up and down that road out there. They must be hundreds of 'em." He slapped his wounded prisoner with the back of his hand and growled, "Walk, dammit, and stand up like a man. You're in the presence of your *Capo*."

Joliet Jake did not seem to know where he was nor why. The old fellow was groaning with a shattered arm and bent almost double, clutching the arm to his belly and making whimpering little sounds of deepest remorse.

Lavallo said to Larry Turk, "Gimme a hand with this—"

Then he saw Bolan, standing tall and stiff against the far wall, and Pete the Hauler promptly lost all interest in his own prisoner. He half ran across the office, drew up beside Giovanni, and gasped, "It's him! It's that rotten shit of a Bolan!"

"It's him all right," the Don replied smugly.

Larry Turk was steering the grievously wounded underboss of the Loop to a lounge chair. Lavallo was eyeing the focal point of all his fears and hatreds, and he must have been thinking that his guy, this rotten bastard, was responsible for all the unspeakable indignities which had befallen Pete the Hauler this day. Don Giovanni was looking like the cat which was just about to dine upon a canary.

And then Pete the Hauler "lost his mind" and forgot where he was and why. He gave an enraged bellow of frustrations released, and "the magnificient fuckup" threw himself upon the object of his pinpointed hatreds, chopping at Bolan with the little revolver and

180

apparently intent on smashing his head in.

And it was all Bolan had needed. He smoothly went inside the attack, turned Lavallo effortlessly around and held him there as a shield. Meanwhile the Belle of the Ball was whisking clear of her sideleather.

Don Gio was throwing lead pointblank into the stiffening and suddenly wracked human shield, and trying to scamper to one side for a better firing angle. Bolan accorded the old man one split second of his attention and a single blast from the Beretta, then he was flinging himself clear of his dying burden and swinging to meet the attack that counted.

Larry Turk was running toward him and blazing away with the .45, and Bolan was aware that at least two of those zinging chunks had carried away parts of his own flesh in their passage.

Bolan caressed the Belle's trigger four times, twice in mid-fling and twice from rolling-prone, and Larry Turk's charge faltered and died. He stood there for a moment giving Bolan the dazed, I-don't-believe-it stare then the Belle spoke once more and an I-believe-it third eye opened at the bridge of Larry Turk's nose and he pitched over backwards, dead in the air.

Bolan rolled across the floor for an inspection of Don Giovanni. The old warrior had a Parabellum in his Nassau-softened belly, and Bolan could see the life draining away from those weary old eyes. The *Capo* coughed and a trickle of blood flowed across the corner of his mouth. He groaned, "Put me in my chair. Let me die with dignity."

Bolan told him, "You'll die as you lived, Gio, in blood and crap up to your neck." Then he got to his feet and went to the lounge where Joliet Jake was shuddering with pain, oblivious to the death scene about him.

181

Bolan bent over him, and something flickered in those pained eyes, and Vecci gasped, "It's *you*, th' telephone guy!"

Bolan said, "Yeh, I've been a lot of guys tonight, Jake. Busy busy busy."

"Well what a hell of a night this turns out to be," the sub*capo* groaned.

Bolan told him, "Count your blessings, Jake," and he stepped away, disengaged and ready to shake that joint.

But then another man ran into the office, the tails of his topcoat flying out behind him, and he halted abruptly at sight of the big guy in the white jumpsuit. The man said, "Oh God."

Bolan thought, *yeah, oh God.* It was a face familiar to millions of Americans around the country, an almost intimate face to anyone who'd ever watched a televised news program or any other national hi-jinks from Chicago. That face had appeared on the covers of *Time* and in countless other magazines and newspapers. Pretty big stuff, this guy.

Bolan felt a bit queasy at his stomach as he glowered at the man and told him, "You got here late, Jim. Or do we call you *City* Jim in this hallowed place?"

The guy was staring at the black blaster in Bolan's clenched fist. In a voice of total resignation he declared, "Okay, let's get it over with."

"Not a chance," Bolan told him. "You'll have to meet your fate in its own time and place, bub."

And then Bolan went away from there, back across the sumptuous office built of terror and savage greed, up the winding iron stairway, and back along the route of entry.

He dropped lightly into the snow at the rear of the building and made for the river, mentally counting and assessing his own wounds, and listening appreciatively to the waning sounds of combat out front. The cops were taking over, and Bolan wished them well, both here and in the inevitable clouted courtrooms just beyond.

He reached his war-wagon and borrowed enough time from flight to tape compresses over the three flesh wounds he'd picked up from Larry the Late Turkeymaker, and then he drove confidently onto the ice and headed upriver.

As the scene for a wipe-out, the big windy city beside the lake had been a real charmer. Bolan quietly and humbly thanked Chicago . . . and he thanked the universe for all kind favors received.

Sure, it mattered who won. And the universe cared.

EPILOGUE

The signboard outside the modest North Side home had been hastily altered to read: LEOPOLD STEIN, LEGAL ADVISOR.

Bolan smiled and punched the doorbell. It was four o'clock in the morning, sure, but the joint was ablaze with lights, and the cute kid who answered the ring was looking as though she could remain awake for another twenty-four hours. Her eyes were glistening as she led him into the living quarters, and she announced, "Daddy, it's the man."

Bolan could not think of kinder words nor a nicer tribute, and he could not imagine a warmer welcome than the six-feet of foxy womanhood who flung herself into his arms.

She checked him out, limb by limb and almost organ by organ, oohing and worrying over the miniscule losses of flesh here and there, and Bolan had to allow them to fuss over the wounds with antiseptics and bandages—and finally he was seated at a big dining table with Jimi on his lap and a heftily-laced cup of coffee in his hand, and he told his host, "I see you changed your shingle outside."

Stein grinned and replied, "The groundhog came out early and failed to see his shadow. To hell with that slime, Mack. I'll never hide from them again."

"Be careful, Leo," Bolan advised him. "The clout machine is probably as strong as ever."

"You forget," the lawyer reminded his guest. "We got the whole report on television, nearly an hour before you toddled in here. I never heard of such a slaughter. Out of the whole hierarchy of the Chicago syndicate, there's nothing but a few lieutenants and one lousy sub*capo* still alive. A guy named Meninghetti is in the clink, also a Drago."

"How about Benny Rocco?" Bolan asked. "And Spanno."

Stein shook his head. "They've seen their last appeals court."

"Okay, I'll scratch them from my book," Bolan murmured. "Uh, I meant what I said about being careful. There's still a lot of dirt in this town, Leo."

"Oh hell, I know that. Tell you what. I'll promise to be as careful as you. Okay?"

Bolan smiled soberly, trusting that the universe would be as concerned for men like Leo Stein as for wildass warriors like Mack Bolan. He realized, however, that the universe cares only for those who care for themselves—and for *it*—and the brief interlude of stolen camaraderie with friends he could trust was about used up.

He got to his feet and made ready for his re-entry into the jungle of survival. He shook hands with his new friends, the Steins, and he pulled Jimi into the office foyer for a private farewell.

"You watch it," he growled, and poured an accumulation of loneliness and pent emotions into that goodbye kiss.

She clung to him and breathlessly asked him, "Where will you go? What will you do now?"

He whispered, "*Down!*"—and she stiffened momentarily in his embrace, then she shivered and clung to him all the more.

"That's where I live, Foxy," he reminded her. "It's home, and the only place I *can* live."

"Well, you watch that beloved flesh, you hear?" she said huskily.

He disengaged from the embrace and went to the door, turned around for a final look, and then he was through the doorway and moving briskly into no-man's-land.

A man moves steadily, he knew, from the womb to the grave. It mattered little where he entered the world or where he left it. What counted was that route between the two. And Mack Bolan's only route lay in the jungle. It was the place where he lived. One day it would be the place for him to die. This was both his character and his fate. The Executioner accepted both . . . as a heritage. He would move forever along the wipeout trail, until the final decision was rendered.

Somewhere, somehow, the whole savage and bloody thing mattered. It was not a senseless game, from which a guy could just disengage any time the going became a little rough.

It was life, and Mack Bolan meant to live his to the bloody, bitter end. This was, simply, the kind of guy he was.

THE EXECUTIONER

The most exciting series ever to explode into print!

Meet Mack Bolan, self-appointed one-man death squad sworn to destroy the Mafia—single-handed! Stung by his devastating attacks, the Families have put out a $100,000 contract on him, and every gun man in the world is welcome to try to collect on it! Bolan is alone, as even the forces of law and order are out to stop his solitary killer crusade.

You won't want to miss a single word of this dynamite series. Check the order form on the last page and get your copies today!

THE BEST IN PAPERBACKS FROM PINNACLE BOOKS!

If you enjoyed this book, you're sure to want the other exciting titles from PINNACLE BOOKS. Here are the highlights of the most intriguing and entertaining paper back books being published today!

TALES FROM THE UNKNOWN, by Arthur Machen. A collection of seventeen perplexing and terrifying stories of supernatural and psychic phenomena by notable writers. **No. P054—95¢**

CIVIL WAR II: The Day It Finally Happened, by Dan Britain. The blacks take over the cities and America hovers on the brink of a racial doomsday. **No. P055—95¢**

FOURTH STREET EAST, by Jerome Weidman. A warm and wonderful book telling the story of Benny Kramer and his boyhood in New York City's Lower East Side in the atmosphere of the twenties. **No. P056—$1.25**

HOW TO MARRY A MARRIED MAN, by Mary English. The indispensable guide book for women who really want to get married—not just play at it! **No. P057—95¢**

THE GROUPSEX SCENE, by John F. Trimble, Ph.D. This new, shocking and intimate account reveals what GroupSex is all about and how it may affect our society—even you! **No. P058—$1.25**

CALLEY: SOLDIER OR KILLER, by Tom Tiede. A Pinnacle Original! Written by prize-winning war correspondent. **No. P065—95¢**

THE VALIANT SAILORS, by V. A. Stuart. A new series—the hero, Phillip Horatio Hazard, more dramatic and more exciting than Hornblower! **No. P060—95¢**

FIRST CONTACT by Damon Knight. 10 masterpieces of science fiction to blow your mind. **No. P062—95¢**

TIMES AND PLACES, by Emily Hahn. The fascinating memoirs of an extraordinary woman . . . her adventures in exciting times and exotic places. Written with gusto, humor and affection. **P063—$1.25**

NAKED, AS AN AUTHOR, by Pietro Di Donato. A collection of short stories by the bestselling author of **Christ in Concrete** and **This Woman.** Exposes the desires and passions of mankind. **P066—95¢**

GUNS FOR GENERAL LI, by Jack Lewis. A superb adventure telling the story of two daredevil soldiers of fortune who undertake—unwillingly—an incredible mission into Red China. **P067—95¢**

HOW TO "MAKE IT" 365 DAYS A YEAR, by Paul Warren. The one indispensable guide for the man-about-town, or the would-be man-about-town. Be more attractive to women—watch your life change! **No. P092—$1.25**

ORDER NOW TO KEEP AHEAD!

To order, check the space next to the books you want, then mail your order, together with cash, check or money order, to: Pinnacle Books, Mail Order Dep't., Box 4347, Grand Central Station, New York, New York 10017.